To Barbara

I hope you e
it — stay warm t_ _ _ _ _
a curl up with a good

Kathleen Anne Barrett

12-4-96

MILWAUKEE WINTERS CAN BE MURDER

MILWAUKEE
WINTERS
CAN BE
MURDER

•

KATHLEEN ANNE
BARRETT

Kathleen Anne Barrett

12-5-94

AVALON BOOKS
THOMAS BOUREGY AND COMPANY, INC.
401 LAFAYETTE STREET
NEW YORK, NEW YORK 10003

PRINTED IN THE UNITED STATES OF AMERICA
ON ACID-FREE PAPER
BY HADDON CRAFTSMEN, SCRANTON, PENNSYLVANIA

To my darling Billy, who brought
me the joy that enabled me to write

Acknowledgments

I wish to acknowledge and thank the following people: my parents, Dr. James M. Barrett and Mary P. Barrett; my brothers, James M. Barrett and Patrick S. Barrett; my sister, Mary Eileen Barrett; my husband, William E. Hoese, and my son, William J. Hoese, for their invaluable insights, encouragement and assistance; Nancy Fullam, Esq., for her unflagging loyalty and promotional assistance; Colleen Hartley, for the use of her elegant name; Jane Ristaino, for a means of escape; Patty Shannon at The Work Station, for her terrific typing; Dann P. Sullivan, for his always fertile ideas; Debra Wojtowski, for her great friendship and encouragement; and Donna Zahorik, for inspiring me to begin.

Chapter One

"**B**eth! What the heck happened?" Emily said as she rushed into my kitchen.

"I don't know a whole lot," I said. "We only talked for a few minutes. She just says Dave was lying on the floor with an empty pill bottle in his hand and there was a suicide note in the typewriter."

"But why would he kill himself?" Emily said. "It doesn't make any sense."

"Well . . . he may not have," I said.

"Huh?"

"He may not have killed himself. Janice is absolutely positive he was murdered."

Emily gaped at me and sat down, nearly missing the chair.

"I don't believe this," she said. "What makes her think Dave was murdered?"

"The suicide note, mostly. She says it's something he never would've written. She didn't tell me what it said but she says there's no way he could've written that note."

Emily squinched up her face.

"Well, she knows her own brother," I said.

"Yeah, maybe." Emily leaned back in her chair, folded her arms across her chest, pursed her lips, and stared at me. Great, I could just see what was coming next.

"Well, come on," she said. "How many people have you heard of who've been murdered with a bottle of pills?"

"Well, I don't know," I said. "No one, I guess. What does that have to do with it?"

"Well, what do you think, some guy just pried open his

1

mouth and shoved the whole bottle of pills down his throat?''
She gave me her favorite look, which I ought to be used to
by now. Disdainful, superior, and *super* condescending. She'll
never say she's superior, mind you. She'll never actually tell
you you're stupid—but the *looks,* let me tell you. It's like
you're the world's biggest idiot.

"I don't know," I said again. "Maybe somebody had a
gun on him and forced him to do it."

"Oh, right. How likely is that?"

"Well, I don't know. Maybe the guy ground the pills up
and put them in his beer or something."

Emily rolled her eyes. "Yeah, *right,*" she said. "It's a good
thing you're not investigating his death."

I shrugged—very nonchalantly—picked up a pencil, and
started doodling. When I looked up, Emily was watching me.

"What's going on?" she said.

"Nothing," I said, trying not to sound defensive. I made a
long chain of ovals curled into a large "S." I looked up again.
She was still watching me. I pursed my lips, put a stem on
the "S," and turned it into a really weird flower.

"Janice says the police think it's a routine suicide, and
they'll only do a routine investigation. She asked me to help
her prove he was murdered, and I said I would."

Emily groaned. "Are you out of your mind? How could
you let her talk you into something like that?"

"Well, what was I supposed to do, just tell her to forget
it?"

"Yes!"

I rolled my eyes and looked away.

"What are you going to do," Emily said, "wrestle the guy
to the ground when you catch him? You don't even weigh
enough to donate blood, for Pete's sake. I mean, you're even
smaller than my nine-year-old niece. You're not . . . my dog
sat on you once and you couldn't even get up, do you remember that?"

I glared at her. "I was eleven years old when that happened."

"Yes. But you were the same size you are now."

I closed my eyes and took a deep breath. "Look," I said. "Let's just drop it, okay?"

"This has got to be the stupidest . . ."

I gave Emily the same you'd-better-shut-up look I like to give my brother—and it worked! I love it when that happens.

It wasn't quite three in the afternoon, but it was black as could be outside. The wind was screaming and throwing ice at my house. Milwaukee was having its third ice storm of the season and it was only December twentieth. Typical. Emily didn't want to drive home so she stayed over. We watched videos, ate some nachos, a bowl of popcorn, a small pizza, and about a dozen of the doughnuts I'd made that morning (no, not all at once). And we talked *ad nauseum* about Phil (Emily's husband) and all the guys we'd ever gone out with. We actually shared a few (no, not at the same time). At two A.M., I put Emily in one of my guest rooms and went to bed. The sound of a salt truck woke me at four, but I went right back to sleep.

My name is Beth Hartley, by the way. I'm forty-two years old, I live on the east side of Milwaukee, and I run my own business doing legal research and writing for other lawyers. We're like ghostwriters. (Actually, we *are* ghostwriters.) Lawyers who don't like writing briefs, or who don't have the time, hire us to do it and then put their own names on the finished product. No one ever knows, and everyone's happy. It's a fun way to make a living. I used to practice law myself, but I really hated it, so I quit when I was thirty-four and started the business. I brought my secretary, Janice Grezinski—she's the one whose brother died—with me, and a few years later I hired Emily Schaeffer (she's a lawyer, too). Emily and I have been friends since the fifth grade.

We work out of my house and we do all of our research at Marquette University or on Lexis. It's great. We do really well, I don't have anyone telling me what to do, and I can set my own hours. There's no back-stabbing and no competition. It's a really nice life.

I inherited my house from my Aunt Sarah, my father's

brother's wife. I hope it doesn't sound like I'm bragging, but this house is really amazing. If you could dream up the perfect house, this would be it. It's on Newberry Boulevard, first of all, which is my favorite street in the whole city, and it's enormous. It has everything you could ever want. A real library, with sliding doors, seven bedrooms, four-and-a-half baths, three fireplaces, and the biggest kitchen you've ever seen.

The outside is really pretty—cream-colored brick with hunter green trim and a multicolored pastel slate roof. There's one of those covered carport things over the driveway which leads back to a four-car garage. I have a big yard, a small interior courtyard (I love that), a screened porch in the back, another second-story porch on the side, and a small third-story balcony. And everything is super fancy. The front door is solid walnut, recessed in a little alcove and surrounded by leaded glass and some kind of frilly gingerbread stuff.

The whole house has a sort of fairy-tale look to it. When I first moved in, Emily asked me what kind of architecture it is. I said, "How the heck should I know?" The only thing I can tell you is it's made of Cream City brick—a really pretty, light brick that's peculiar to Milwaukee. Most people assume the name has something to do with milk or beer foam, when they first hear about it, but it doesn't. It's just called that because of the color. (It comes from the sulphate of sulphur in the clay, whatever that means.) It always looks clean and cheery, and Milwaukee's well known for it, so it's kind of neat having a house made out of it.

It took me months to stop feeling like I had to dress up just to live here. I was embarrassed to put my beat-up old Honda in the garage. I felt like I should've had something more elegant, like a Mercedes or a Porsche (more like a Mercedes *and* a Porsche). I'm still not entirely used to it all and it's been more than five years now.

My whole family still lives in Milwaukee, which is nice. My dad's a retired lawyer and my mom stayed home to take care of us. They're in their late sixties now, but they're both in pretty good shape. My brother, Mike, is thirty-eight, unmarried, and runs his own business computerizing people's office records or something like that. My sister Ann is thirty-six. She's married to a guy named Don (a real weirdo, if you ask me), and has three kids (ten, seven, and five). She stays home to take care of them and does a great job, I think. I was married twice, but I don't want to talk about it.

At nine the next morning, Emily came in and woke me up.

"I'm going to Marquette," she said. "The roads are clear."

I squinted. "How do you know?"

"I had the radio on; I've been up since eight. I made you some coffee."

"Mmm, thanks," I said. "You coming back?"

"I don't know," she said. "It depends on how much I get done."

I lay in bed for a while and groaned, then finally got up and took a shower. I put on jeans and a sweatshirt and went downstairs. When I walked into the kitchen, I drew in my breath.

Sometime during the night, while I was sound asleep, my house had been transported by the ice storm to another galaxy, a magical world of shimmering, quivering glass. Through my bay window, I watched sun fairies play and dance, leaving sparkles and diamonds on every branch. My yard was a masterpiece of frozen perfection and light.

I poured myself some coffee, and before I had a chance to take a sip, my bell rang. I put the cup on the table and went to the door.

It was Janice. I put my hand out and touched her arm.

"Janice," I said. "Come in."

She didn't move. I had to draw her in and close the door.

"Let me have your coat," I said. "Come and have some coffee."

She shook her head, her eyes lowered to the floor. "I came to work," she said in a barely audible whisper.

"You don't have to work," I said. I touched her arm again, and tried to get her to look at me.

"I want to," she said.

I took a deep breath, not knowing what to say. "Okay," I said, for lack of anything better.

She walked toward the library.

"Janice?" I said. She turned around.

"Why don't you come in the kitchen for a while before you start? I have coffee, and I made doughnuts yesterday." I lifted an eyebrow and gave her a little smile.

She stood there for a moment, then smiled back. "Okay," she said.

I pulled out a chair for her, and got another mug and some plates from the cupboard. I poured her some coffee, took cream from the refrigerator, and set a plate with a half-dozen doughnuts in the middle of the table.

When I sat down and looked at her face, I almost started crying right then, but I managed to control myself for the time being. She looked so awful—so haggard and beaten up. Her skin sagged around her eyes and mouth, her color was pallid, almost gray, and she had dark patches under her eyes. She's only thirty-one, and she usually looks no more than maybe twenty-five. But that day she looked almost ancient. It was the look in her eyes that upset me the most. A sort of flat, lifeless stare, like she was tuning out her pain and the rest of the world along with it.

"How are you doing?" I said gently.

She made an attempt to smile and shrugged. Then her lip started to quiver and she put her hand against her mouth as a wash of tears spilled from her eyes. It caught me by surprise, and the tears I'd been holding back just poured out and wouldn't stop. My sister always says I make things worse for people when I do that. But at least I care, you know?

After we both calmed down a bit, Janice wiped her eyes and let out a sigh. She cradled the coffee cup in her hands and pressed the warm mug against her forehead.

I smiled. "You want a doughnut?" I said.

She looked at the plate I'd put in the center of the table and shook her head. "Maybe later," she said.

We sat in silence for several minutes, just looking out the window.

"I have to find out who did this to him, Beth," she said a little later. "I know he didn't kill himself, I just know it."

I put my hand on her arm and squeezed gently. "We will," I said. "I promise. We won't give up until we do."

She rested her eyes on my face for a few moments. "But how?" she said. "How are we going to do it?"

I wasn't really ready for that question. I hadn't actually thought about it yet.

"Uh . . . well," I said. "We could start by interviewing people, I guess. People he knew. See if anyone knew about anything weird going on in his life."

Janice's face brightened considerably.

"We could make a list of people we could talk to," I said.

"Okay," she said. "Let's do it."

"You mean you want to do it now?" I said, showing my surprise.

"Yes, I do," she said with an emphatic nod.

"Okay." I went into the library and got a legal pad from my desk.

I wrote *People We Need To Talk To* at the top of a page, and underlined it twice. I raised my eyebrows at Janice. "Any ideas?" I asked.

"Put down Jake Grossman," she said. "His roommate."

I wrote *1. Jake Grossman—roommate.* "I take it he wasn't there when you found him, huh?"

Janice shook her head. "No, and Mom's been trying to call him ever since but he never answers."

"So, as far as you know, he doesn't even know about it?"

"Oh, he probably does," she said. "The police would've told him by now. We gave them his name and everything."

"Do you know where he's from?" I asked.

"Cedarburg, I think."

"Okay, anyone else?"

"His girlfriend," Janice said. "Her name's Laura . . . something. I never actually met her, though."

Janice had a sort of injured look on her face. Or maybe it was annoyance.

"What's the matter?" I said.

"Oh, I don't know," she said. "I just had the impression he didn't want me to meet her."

"Hmm. Well, I'm sure you'll get to meet her now. Who else?"

"The doctor he worked for, I guess—Dr. Chapman. I think his first name's Anthony. His office is on Brady Street."

"I thought Dave didn't work during the school year."

"Well, this was a special case. It was only temporary and it was the same kind of work he wanted to do when he graduated."

"What was he planning to do?" I said.

"Put peoples' office records on computer and organize everything for them. He was going to start his own business."

"Hey, that's exactly what my brother Mike does. He has his own business, too. Weird—they would've been doing the same thing."

Janice didn't respond, but she looked like I'd flicked a little dart in her heart. There, I'd done it again. I had to go and open my big mouth. I hadn't thought about it before I said it, but it was like I was rubbing what Dave might've been right in her face. My brother Mike says I *never* think before I talk. I just jump right in and say everything that's on my mind. Which is why, he said once, I have very little to say on any subject. I won't tell you what I said back.

"What about his other friends?" I asked Janice, hoping to divert her attention from my insensitivity. "Did you ever meet any of them?"

"Just Jake," she said.

I tapped my pen on the table a few times, and scowled. "Can you think of anyone else?" I asked.

"Not really," she said.

"Well, what did he do with his free time? Did he have any hobbies or anything?"

"He was a wrestler," Janice said. "He was on the team at Marquette. He was always in some competition or meet or whatever they call it."

"Do you know who his coach was, or any of the guys he wrestled with?"

"No, sorry," she said, shaking her head. "I only went to watch him once. It was pretty gross."

I laughed. "Yeah, I know what you mean.

"What did he usually talk about when you saw him?" I said.

"His business, mostly. He'd been planning it for a long time. It was just about all he ever talked about lately."

"Was he going to do it alone?"

"Yes . . . well, he wasn't going to have any partners, but he was thinking of having some sort of investor for a while. But then the guy backed out."

"When did that happen?" I asked.

"I don't know, a long time ago. Like over a year, maybe?"

"Do you know who the guy was?"

Janice shook her head. "It was another student, I think, but I never knew his name."

"Okay." I gazed out the window and thought some more. This was harder than I'd expected it to be. I felt like I didn't know what to ask, or what to do with the answers once I got them. None of these people could possibly have anything to do with Dave's death, could they?

"Didn't you mention to me once that Dave saw a cardiologist?" I said. "What's his name?"

"Uh . . . shoot, I can't remember. The empty bottle of pills was Dave's heart medication. I'll have to ask Mom what the doctor's name is."

"How's she doing, by the way?"

Janice's face said "Don't ask," but she answered anyway. "Who knows?" she said. "It's hard to tell with Mom. If you ask me, she's either in complete shock or she's crazy or something. You'd never even know anything had happened to her."

"What do you mean?" I said with a frown.

"She acts just like normal. She doesn't even talk about it, she doesn't cry, and she doesn't act upset. She just cleans the house all day long and then goes to work just like usual. It's like she doesn't even care."

I gave Janice a sympathetic smile. "Maybe she really is in shock," I said. "Maybe this is the only way she can cope with it all. It might be too painful for her to acknowledge it right now. You know what I mean?''

Janice hesitated a moment. ''Well, maybe,'' she said, a little grudgingly.

I had a sudden thought. ''Does your mom know we're doing this?'' I said.

''Yeah, don't worry, she doesn't care. She didn't even say anything when I told her.''

''Do you think she'd mind talking to me?''

Janice gave me a rather sharp glance, and lowered her eyes. ''Well, I don't know; you'd better let me ask her first.''

''Okay,'' I said, a little confused by her reaction.

Now what? Friends, hobbies. School! ''How was he doing in school?'' I said.

Janice smiled. ''He always got straight As,'' she said. ''All his life.''

''Wow. Must be nice, huh?''

''Yeah, right,'' Janice said.

''So tell me about Jake,'' I said. ''How'd he end up living with Dave? Was he a computer major too?''

''No, he wasn't a computer major. He doesn't even know how to use one,'' she said with a derisive laugh. ''I think he's in Soc, or something like that.''

I considered reminding her that I don't know how to use a computer, either, but I decided against it—too embarrassing to mention.

''Where'd Dave meet him then?'' I said.

''He was living with someone else,'' she said, ''but the guy moved out so he put an ad in the paper and Jake answered it.''

''Do you like him?''

''Who, Jake? Oh, sure. He's nice.''

''Did he and Dave get along all right?''

''Yeah, I guess,'' Janice said, frowning. ''Why? You don't think he did it, do you?'' She seemed shocked that I would even consider such a possibility.

''No, it's not that,'' I said. ''I'm just trying to find out as much as I can about anyone who knew him, that's all.'' I was trying to fight it, but I felt a little resentful that I was having to defend myself for asking questions I thought I needed to ask. After all, Janice was the one who'd begged me to do this in the first place.

That's when I remembered the suicide note.

"Oh, tell me about the suicide note," I said. "Why are you so sure Dave didn't write it?"

"Because it doesn't make any sense," she said. "It says he was taking his own life because he couldn't pay his debts, and because he couldn't face prosecution for the bomb scares. But he doesn't have any debts, and they weren't going to prosecute him for the bomb scares."

I was totally confused. "Bomb scares?" I said. "What are you talking about? What bomb scares?"

Janice blushed a deep pink. "Remember all those bomb threats they had at Marquette during finals last week?"

"Yeah?"

She took a deep breath and let it out. "Dave was the one who called them in."

I stared at her in disbelief. "What? Why in the world would he do that?" I said.

"I don't know," Janice said, lowering her eyes and her voice. "He wouldn't tell me. But he did tell me they weren't going to prosecute him," she added. "He knew that for sure. We were talking about it the night before he died."

"Wow, I see what you mean. What about the debts? Are you sure about that, too?"

"Well, yeah. The only debt he would've had was his school loan, but he wouldn't even have to be paying that yet."

"I thought you were paying his tuition."

"Well, I was paying for the rest," she said. "Whatever the loan didn't take care of."

I nodded, thinking hard. Maybe Janice was right. It wouldn't make any sense for Dave to have written that suicide note. Maybe it really was written by someone else. Well, in that case, I already knew what I was going to do next.

Chapter Two

Just then, Mrs. Gunther walked in. What perfect timing. She could keep Janice company while I did what I had to do. Mrs. Gunther is my housekeeper, and I love her. As far as I'm concerned, she's a part of my family. In fact, my whole family knows her. She worked for my Aunt Sarah since I was a little kid and I kept her on after Aunt Sarah died. My aunt had Mrs. Gunther in every Monday, Wednesday, and Friday for twenty-five years, and now, so do I. With a house this big, it takes her the whole three days just to get through all the rooms.

I really like having her here. We can talk about almost anything, and we've helped each other through some pretty unhappy times. She's a widow, fifty-five years old, and she lives in the same neighborhood she's lived in all her life (only a few miles from me). Her sister Erma lives three blocks away from her. Erma's not too well off financially, but she refuses to move in with Mrs. Gunther. She won't even accept any money from her. She says she doesn't want to be a burden to anybody.

Aunt Sarah left Mrs. Gunther quite a lot of money but Mr. Gunther got very sick soon after that so they went through it pretty quickly. He had to be put in a nursing home and their insurance didn't cover it. She still has the life insurance from him, and a good income from me, though, so she lives pretty comfortably—which makes her feel all the worse about Erma.

She was wearing a blue flowered dress that day with a pink scarf holding back her hair. She makes all her own clothes and wears flowered cotton dresses all year-round. It's like looking at a big flower garden in the middle of winter.

12

When Mrs. Gunther spotted Janice, who had her back to her, she gave me a quizzical look.

I answered with a little shrug, and a sad face.

Mrs. Gunther walked over to the table and sat in the chair next to Janice's. Janice turned, took one look at Mrs. Gunther, and started sobbing. I was a bit surprised, but maybe it was a good thing, I thought. It would do her good to get it all out.

"You go right ahead and cry, honey," Mrs. Gunther said. "You just cry as long and as hard as you want to." She folded Janice in her arms and rocked her gently, back and forth, like a little baby. That made me start crying again, and I quickly left the room.

I went into the library, closed the doors, and sat down at my desk. I closed my eyes for a while and just sat, listening to myself breathe. This whole thing was so emotionally draining. I got up, opened the drapes, and sat down again. The sun reflected off the ice on the trees, creating a curious mottled pattern on the books lining the walls. There must be a thousand of them. I tried counting them once but I got tired and quit.

I leaned back in my chair.

What in the world happened to Dave?

And why in the world did he make those bomb threats? It wasn't just a few, either. The paper said it was almost twenty over a period of three days. Really weird.

He'd always gotten straight As, Janice said. Until now, maybe? He was flunking out for the first time in his life and he couldn't handle it, so he . . . what? Made a desperate attempt to postpone his exams by making a bunch of bomb threats? Somehow, that didn't seem likely. And even if it were true, how would it tie in with his death?

Well, time to get to work, I decided. I got the number for the computer sciences building at Marquette, and dialed the main office. A woman with a sort of trembly voice answered.

"Hi," I said. "My name is . . . Janice. Janice Grezinski. My little brother, Dave, was a computer sciences major at Marquette."

"Oh," she said. "Yes." I could tell by the sound of her voice that she'd recognized the name.

"He died last week, though," I said in a sad voice.

"Oh, yes, dear, I know," she said. "Please accept my condolences."

"Thank you," I said. "I know this is probably an unusual request and I don't want to put you to any trouble . . ."

"It's no trouble at all, dear. How may I help you?" she said.

"Well, I'd really like to talk to Dave's teachers," I said, "but I don't know who they are. I don't suppose you'd have a record of that."

"I'm sure I can get that information for you," she said. "Why don't you give me your number, dear, and I'll call you right back."

"Thank you," I said, after I'd recited the number.

"It's no trouble at all, dear."

"Oh, his wrestling coach," I said as she was about to hang up. "I'd really like to talk to his wrestling coach. Wrestling meant so much to Davy."

"Well . . . all right, dear," she said. "I'll do my best."

I turned off my answering machine and waited. Ten minutes later, I had the names and office numbers of all of his teachers and the name and home phone number of his wrestling coach. I couldn't believe it.

I sat back in my chair and grinned. Ha. This was fun.

Okay, next step. Go to Marquette and talk to his teachers.

I walked back toward the kitchen and Janice was heading for the library with two doughnuts in her hands.

"Feel any better?" I said.

She nodded and smiled. She really did look better. Most of the tension had left her face.

"I was thinking of going to Marquette to talk to some of Dave's teachers to see if I can find anything out about this bomb threat business. You want to come with me?" I said.

Janice hesitated for a moment. "No, I can't," she said.

"That's okay," I said with a smile. "I didn't really think

you'd want to but I wanted to make sure. I'll talk to you when I get back. You going to be all right?''

"Yeah," she said. "Thanks." She gestured with one of the doughnuts. "Next time, leave the calories out, okay?"

I laughed. "I'll try. Just eat the holes."

She smiled and I watched her as she walked into the library. Janice is always worrying about her weight. She's really cute, though, and she's not overweight at all. So what if she's not model-thin. Who wants to look like a stick, anyway, right?

The sun was bright, the sky blue and cloudless. The roads were clear, but every tree and bush, even some of the cars, were covered with a thick layer of ice. It looked like something out of a science-fiction movie.

Marquette University is located in downtown Milwaukee between Eleventh and maybe Twentieth streets, about a mile down from the start of the shopping district. It doesn't have a sprawling, wooded campus like you see in most of those college brochures, although there's a really nice tree in front of the language building. The building's pretty neat, too. It's all white, with oblong octagonal things all over it. It looks kind of like a honeycomb with windows. I mean that as a compliment.

I hope you don't get the wrong idea. I really do love Marquette. I spent a lot of years there and I'm very attached to it. It's a Jesuit university with just about every major you could possibly want. People come from all over the world to go there, which is kind of neat. And the campus does look a lot better than it used to. They've put up some attractive new buildings recently, with some pretty decent landscaping, too.

I found a parking space near the bursar's office, which is kitty-corner from the law school on Eleventh and Wisconsin. Three of Dave's teachers had offices in the Cudahy Math and Computer Science building, one in Lalumière (the language building), and one in Wehr Life Sciences. The closest was computer sciences.

Cudahy Math and Computer Science is one of the positive, relatively new additions to the campus. I absolutely love the lobby. It has a high atrium with two staircases going up in different directions at one of the entrances, and a single staircase at the other. A huge seal of the university is inlaid in the marble floor. (That's my favorite part.)

A lot of intelligent-looking computer types were milling about. For all they knew, I was one of them. I mean, you can't detect computer illiteracy at a glance—or can you? I tried the offices for all three of Dave's computer teachers, but they were all gone for the semester. Darn. I left, trying to look like I had bits and bytes on my mind, and headed for Lalumière.

Lalumière is less than a block away, right across from the old student union. Dave was taking French I from a Dr. Jardin, and, voilà, she was there. Dr. Françoise Jardin had finely sculpted features, honey-blond hair worn in a French twist (why wasn't I surprised?), and brilliant green eyes. She was thin, and petite, and wore a pale pink knit dress with a print scarf in a deep shade of rose around her neck. She was so delicate, and elegant, and beautiful, I couldn't believe it. I tried my best not to stare. I told her who I was and explained why I was there.

"I'm sorry," she said, "but I did not know Monsieur Grezinski." She gave the Polish surname a mellifluous French lilt. I smiled at that and she gave me a puzzled look.

We talked for a few minutes. It seems she didn't require attendance (although she took it) and Dave only showed up for the exams. Her final was not disrupted by a bomb threat, and she really couldn't tell me anything about the incident that I didn't already know. Oh, well. Four strikes out of four, so far.

My final stop was Wehr Life Sciences. Dave was also taking Biology I. Languages and science must have been his least favorite subjects so he saved them for the end. I know what that's like. I did the same thing with speech and history. Yuck.

I took the long way and cut through the chemistry building for old times' sake, entering the biology building through the back door. Dr. Higgins' office was on the second floor, room 207. The door was closed but I could hear someone tapping away on a manual typewriter. It was the only sign of life I'd detected in the building.

I knocked on the door and someone said, "Enter." I opened the door and went in.

Dr. Higgins was about forty-five years old, with very little hair and hazel eyes. He looked at me and smiled in an easy, laid-back way and said, "Can I help you?" in a voice to match. I liked him.

I was just about to answer when I spotted his tropical fish tank at the back of the room. I drew in my breath and just stared. It was a vision. Vibrant blues and yellows, oranges and reds, moved gracefully through clear, filtered water and slowly swaying sea plants.

"Beautiful, aren't they," he said after a moment.

"Oh, they're gorgeous," I said. "I could watch them for hours."

He laughed. "I've done that myself, on occasion."

I introduced myself, and told him my reason for being there.

He arched his eyebrows and sat up straight. "How would you like a Coke?" he said.

"Sure," I said with a laugh.

"Have a seat," he said. "I'll be right back."

After he left, I went back to the fish tank to take a closer look. There's something about fish, especially ones as beautiful as those, that calms me down. I can actually feel my body relax as I'm watching them.

On the wall to the left of the tank were two drawings, obviously composed by a child. They looked like circles with little lines and dots in them.

"Admiring my daughter's artwork, I see," Dr. Higgins said from behind me. I turned and grinned.

"Do you mind my asking what they are?" I said with a look of apology.

"Actinosphaeria and paramecia. Invertebrate protozoa."

I smiled and looked impressed. I only drew houses and stick men when I was a child. Maybe a cat every once in a while.

"My daughter, Kelly, wanted me to teach her some biology so I told her that actinosphaeria eat paramecia. I even brought her down to the lab and showed her some specimens under the microscope, but she didn't like seeing one eat the other so she drew them in separate petri dishes. The one on the left's the paramecia, in case you're interested,'' he said with a lop-sided smile.

Dr. Higgins handed me a Coke and I sat down in the pale green molded plastic chair in front of his desk. He sat in his own chair behind it.

He rested his eyes on my face for a few moments, and nodded. ''So, how can I help you?'' he said. ''I'm afraid I didn't know Mr. Grezinski personally. I have a rather large class—seven hundred and fifty this semester.''

''Wow,'' I said. ''Do you take attendance?''

He laughed. ''No, not anymore. It wasn't worth the trouble. Now I just tell them if they don't attend the lectures they'll probably flunk, and they usually show up.''

''Yeah, I guess I would, too.''

''What sort of information are you looking for?'' he asked.

''I'm trying to find out why Dave made all those bomb threats,'' I said. ''I think it might be related to his murder somehow because they were mentioned in the suicide note. His sister, Janice, says he's gotten straight As all his life, though, so why would he interrupt his exams that way?''

Dr. Higgins took a swig of Coke and set down the bottle with a tap. He raised his index finger. ''Two points,'' he said. ''One, none of the disrupted exams were postponed long enough to do him any good even if he had planned it to get more study time. And two, he didn't make any of the threats during his own exams, anyway. Every one of them was made during an exam in a course he wasn't taking.''

''Huh, how strange,'' I said with a frown.

Dr. Higgins raised his eyebrows and nodded. ''He caused a heck of a lot of damage, though.''

''What do you mean, damage?''

''This is just a for-instance,'' he said, raising his index finger again. ''We had a Ph.D. candidate, working on an experiment in one of the labs—the subject of his thesis—and they vacated the building. He refused to leave. They had to carry him out." Dr. Higgins shook his head. "The experiment was ruined. He dropped out of the Ph.D. program and had to be hospitalized for depression."

"Oh, my gosh," I said. "That's awful. But why couldn't he just rerun the experiment?"

Dr. Higgins let out a big sigh. "Well, it wasn't that simple," he said. "The material required for the experiment is particularly difficult to obtain, and it's used up in the process. To start over would have set him back, who knows how long. He'd already been working on the degree for five years because of some earlier problems and I guess this was the last straw for him. His heart just went out of it."

"When was he hospitalized for depression?" I asked.

"The day before yesterday. Why?"

I shrugged. "I'm just curious," I said. "Would you mind telling me his name?"

Dr. Higgins shot me a quick look of annoyance. "I'm sorry, I can't do that," he said. "He's already suffered quite enough. I can assure you, Ms. Hartley, you're barking up the wrong tree with that one."

"Okay," I said with a sigh. I was already running out of ideas. "Do you know anything at all about Dave?" I said.

Dr. Higgins shook his head. "Only what I read in the *Tribune* about the bomb threats," he said.

"Do you have any theories about why he did it?" I asked.

"I'm sorry," Dr. Higgins said. "I wish I could help you. As far as I know, he never revealed his reasons."

"Well, thanks, Dr. Higgins," I said, and stood up to leave.

"Oh, do you know how he got caught?" I suddenly remembered to ask.

Dr. Higgins snorted a laugh. "He was making one of his calls from a pay phone in one of the dorms," he said. "Another student overheard him and turned him in."

I rolled my eyes. "Well, thanks, again," I said. "You've been a big help." I offered Dr. Higgins my hand.

"Glad I could be of service," he said. "Feel free to call me if you have any more questions." We exchanged numbers, and I asked him to do the same if something else occurred to him.

Well, at least I was getting somewhere. I didn't know much yet, but it was better than nothing. There was something very strange about that prank of his. It just had to tie in somehow. I was disappointed that Dr. Higgins hadn't even met Dave, though. What I really needed was to talk to someone who knew him well. His *mother*—she was the one I'd talk to next. It turned out to be a good plan, too. I picked up some pretty useful tidbits of information from her, later that night.

It was just a little before noon when I left Dr. Higgins's office, and I was starving. I stopped at McDonald's, got Janice a Big Mac, a regular hamburger for myself, and a fish sandwich for Mrs. Gunther. The ice was beginning to melt and the otherworldly look was dripping away. I went through the drive-thru along with about two dozen others, and didn't get home until almost one.

I poked my head in the library when I came in. Janice was hard at work, typing even faster than her usual eighty words per minute. Boy, I wish I could do that. The best I've ever managed is about thirty words per minute, and that's with a whole ton of mistakes. When I first started my business, I had Janice typing on my old electric typewriter, but then the "G" broke so I splurged and got the computer. Just try writing an appellate brief sometime without using any words with the letter "G" in them.

"McDonald's delivery," I said in a singsong voice.

Janice turned around and grinned. "Hey, great," she said. "Thanks."

I found Mrs. Gunther upstairs and we all sat down at the kitchen table. I suddenly remembered Emily with a twinge of guilt. "Emily didn't come back, did she?" I said.

Mrs. Gunther put on a snooty face and said, "No, Ms. Schaeffer has not graced us with her presence."

Janice and I looked at each other and laughed.

"How's Erma doing?" I said to Mrs. Gunther.

"She's feeling a little better," Mrs. Gunther said. "She has her monthly checkup next week, so we'll see."

"What's wrong with her?" Janice said.

Mrs. Gunther threw up her arms. "Honey, what isn't wrong with her? She's got arthritis so bad she can hardly dress herself, she's got fifty pounds too much, she's got high blood pressure, she's diabetic, and now they think it's her thyroid."

"Good grief," Janice said.

We kept up the same sort of chitchat for a good half-hour, and then went back to work. When Janice and I reached the library, I told her about my conversation with Dr. Higgins.

"Do you have any idea at all why he'd do that for classes he wasn't even taking?" I asked.

She looked at me with a mixture of anxiety and confusion. "I really don't," she said.

We worked in relative silence for the rest of the afternoon. At four, Janice started packing up. I looked over at her and smiled.

"I want to go see Mom before she takes off for work," she said. "Do you mind?"

I shook my head and smiled, then had a sudden thought. "Do you think she'd mind if I came to the restaurant and talked to her tonight?" I said.

Janice wrinkled her brow. "Let me ask her and I'll call you," she said. "Is it okay if I let you know about tomorrow, too?"

"Sure," I said. "I only want you working if you want to do it. As far as I'm concerned, you can have all the time you need. I mean that."

She gave me an appreciative smile. "Thanks," she said.

After Janice left, I ate a banana and a mango and made myself a cup of tea. Mrs. Gunther was gone, too, so I brought my work into the kitchen and continued writing there.

I actually do quite a lot of work in my kitchen. It's one of my favorite rooms in the house. I'm not nuts about the wallpaper—it's a sort of dingy green with teapots and big spoons all over it—but I like everything else. The table's big, over six feet long, so I have lots of room to spread out. It's made

of farmhouse pine, with a really nice finish, and there are two
china cabinets to match. It's the kitchen of my dreams, except
for the wallpaper, of course.

I was working on a brief that I'd promised to a client by
Christmas Eve, and I was about two-thirds of the way through.
I arranged all my stuff on the table and got to it.

At five-thirty, the phone rang.

"Hi, it's me," Janice said. "Mom says stop by any time
but if you come around ten she'll be able to talk better. It's
pretty dead by then."

"Great. Thanks," I said. "Did you decide about tomorrow?"

"Yeah," Janice said. "I think I'll spend the day with Mom,
if you don't mind."

"I was hoping you'd say that," I said.

I told Janice I'd see her tomorrow night at the wake, and
hung up. I made arrangements then for a temporary typist for
the next day, and went back to the brief. At seven-thirty, I
was through. I called Emily and asked if she could come a
little early the next day, so she'd be in the house while the
temp was here. I had some research to do, and it had to be
done tomorrow. She said she would.

Good. That was taken care of. I NordicTracked for twenty
minutes, showered and changed, and went to work on another
brief. This one was due several days after Christmas. I worked
for another hour, put everything away, and called the weather.

Ten above. Hey, downright balmy. You think I'm kidding,
don't you? I'm telling you, these Milwaukee winters are absolute murder. Between December and March, anything above
zero is sheer heaven. It's not as bad as it sounds, though.
There's plenty to do here to make the months go by. It's
actually kind of fun. We have ice- and snow-sculpting events
every year, and there's always cross-country skiing or outdoor
ice skating at quite a few of the public parks (we have a *lot*
of parks). You can go downhill skiing, too, at the nearby
slopes (manmade, of course, but who really cares?). Or, if
you're a real outdoors wimp, you can skate inside at the Pettit
National Ice Center. I've watched Olympic trials and World

Cup speed skating there, too. You can even watch the athletes practice. It's pretty cool (yes, in more ways than one).

My favorite winter sport is cross-country skiing, though— gliding through the woods at Whitnall Park after a huge snowstorm, when everything is still pure white and glistening in the sun. It's especially beautiful when the creek is still flowing. The running water melts the snow that fell on top of it and you see this gurgling, sparkling stream poking through the mounds of surrounding snow. It's such a gorgeous sight, and so peaceful, too. You really have to see it to appreciate it. It makes you feel like you've been let in on a special secret of nature. Well, no winter fun and frolics for me that night, though. I had a murder to solve.

Marge, Janice's mom, is a waitress at a truck stop right off of I-94, about halfway to Racine. She started working there about twenty years ago, right after Janice's father abandoned them. In all that time, she's never filed for divorce. Janice says Marge is still hoping he'll come back. Now, why would she want him? That's what I'd like to know. Janice was ten when he left, but Dave wasn't even old enough to remember him. He actually showed up once, about three years ago, and then took off again the next day. Janice and Dave didn't even have a chance to see him. What a jerk. Wouldn't it be something if he showed up at the funeral?

The ice and snow that had melted during the day was frozen solid now, forming jagged ruts where tires had moved through the slush. The sand crews were out but the roads were still treacherous. I took my time, even though I'd be late, and got there at a quarter after ten. The parking lot was empty with the exception of two semis, both of which were unoccupied but still running.

This restaurant isn't much to look at, I'm afraid. The outside is nothing but a big white box with a neon sign saying EAT, only most of the "E" is missing so it looks more like AT. I don't think the restaurant even has a name.

The interior is decorated in a manner consistent with the exterior. White Formica-topped booths and tables, white chairs with chrome legs, plain white counter with white stools, and nothing on the walls. They're white, too. So is Marge's uniform. So are the menus. Boy, is it boring.

The only customers in the place were two guys sitting in a booth in a far corner. They looked at me when I came in. One said something to the other and they both laughed uproariously. Ha, ha.

Marge smiled when she saw me. "Ignore them," she said.

I gave her a halfhearted smile.

"Cup of tea with lemon?" she said.

I nodded and took a seat at the counter. Marge set the tea in front of me, and handed me a paper napkin from the dispenser.

"I was worried about you, Beth. You shouldn't be out there in this weather. That road's like a skating rink."

"Yeah, I know," I said. "I probably wouldn't have come if I'd known how bad it was going to be."

Marge looked at me for a few moments. "How does Janice seem to you?" she said.

I shrugged with one shoulder. "Okay, I guess. She wanted to work today and I think it helped a little."

Marge nodded.

I took a sip of tea, purposely stalling. I'd driven all the way out there to talk to her and now I was hesitating. It seemed ridiculous. Here it was only a few days after her son's death and I was planning to bombard her with questions about his life. She knew why I'd come, though, so I could hardly get out of it.

"Would you mind if I ask you some questions about Dave?" I said in a tentative voice.

Marge shook her head. "No, that's fine with me," she said. "Just start right in."

I took a deep breath. "Okay," I said. "Just let me know when you want me to stop."

Marge gave me a faint smile and nodded.

"Janice said you were trying to reach his roommate. Did you have any luck?" I said.

"No, I didn't," Marge said. "Seems awfully strange to me.

You'd think he'd have called me, just to express his condolences if nothing else.''

"Well, I'm sure we'll see him tomorrow night," I said.

Marge shrugged, and made a face like she didn't care.

"Did you ever meet him?" I said.

"Oh, yes. I met him all right."

"What did you think of him?"

Marge raised her eyebrows. "To tell you the truth, he's not quite polite enough to suit me. But I suppose none of them are nowadays. That boy's never said two words to me, in all the time I've known him. Of course, I wasn't over there at the apartment all that often, now that I think of it. Not very polite, though. I'll have to say it. He really isn't very polite.''

I tried to keep from smiling. Marge likes to make sure you get the point, whenever she has one.

"Did he seem like he got along with Dave?" I asked.

"Well, now, I really couldn't say much about that, although there was a time Dave was talking about moving to another place. When I asked him why, he just said he wanted more space. But that place was plenty big enough for the two of them. I had a feeling it was something else, but he never said.''

"So he never complained to you about Jake?"

"Well, no, but it wasn't his way, you know. He wouldn't have said; even if there was something, he just wouldn't have said.''

I nodded, wondering if I should ask her to clarify that. I decided not to bother.

Marge peered into my cup. "How about a refill?" she asked.

"Sure, thanks," I said.

She filled the cup with hot water and put another tea bag and two lemon wedges on the saucer.

She looked tired. Marge is forty-eight, I think, but she looks quite a bit older. She has the same cute face as Janice, though. Same bright brown eyes, tiny nose, and sort of a little kid's smile.

"Did you ever meet Dave's girlfriend?" I asked.

She frowned.

"Laura?" I said.

Marge made the equivalent of a shrug with her mouth. "No, I can't say that I have," she said. "This is the first I ever heard of her."

"Well, it probably wasn't very serious," I said. "Did you ever meet any of his girlfriends?"

"Oh, sure," she said. "He'd bring a girl home every now and again."

"How about his other friends? Guys, I mean. Did he have any he hung around with from your neighborhood?"

Marge pursed her lips. "Well, there was John Stachowski," she said. "But they moved away about ten years ago."

I smiled. Just then, one of the men in the booth belched so loudly it made me jump. Marge yelled over to them to keep the noise down and we both laughed.

"You sure it doesn't bother you, my asking you all these questions?" I said.

She gave me a weak smile. "No, Beth, it's just fine, really. I know you're just trying to help. I'm grateful for anything you can do. Just ask away."

"Okay," I said. "How often did you see Dave during the school year?"

She shrugged. "Twice a month, maybe three times. He'd come Sundays for dinner or Saturdays sometimes he'd help around the house. There's a lot I can't do myself and I can't afford to hire anyone. He wasn't a stranger, that's for sure."

"Did he come any less often recently?" I said.

Marge thought for a few moments before she responded. "Well, come to think of it, I guess he did. I'd be expecting him and he'd call and say he couldn't make it. He always said it was schoolwork, though. He was a good student, I'll give him that."

"Did he seem any different to you lately? Did he act strange in any way?"

"No, no stranger than usual," she said. "He always was a bit odd, though. I used to say if I didn't know better I'd think he was somebody else's."

I laughed and took a sip of tea. "What did he usually talk about when you saw him?" I said a few moments later.

Marge let out a deep sigh, and shook her head. "Whatever crazy scheme he had going at the time," she said. "He had a lot of big plans, that one, just like his father. Jerry was sure he'd be a millionaire by the time he was thirty, can you believe that? He didn't know what to do with himself when he didn't make it. I always worried Dave would end up the same way. He was smart as a whip, but he could come up with the most fool-minded, harebrained ideas. You'd think he didn't have an ounce of sense in his head. He wasted more money trying to make money than anybody I ever knew—even his father."

I raised my eyebrows, and wrote *greedy, super intelligent, but very poor judgment?* on my notepad, making sure Marge didn't see it.

Just then, the guys in the booth got up to leave. Oh, darn. They walked by and the tall one looked me over, tried his best to memorize all my parts, and winked. Oh, yuck.

Marge asked me if I wanted another cup of tea and I said yes but I needed to go to the bathroom first. I'd been waiting for half an hour because I didn't want to have to walk past the dashing duo in the back. It was already past eleven and I wanted to get going pretty soon. I only had a few more questions in mind, anyway. If I thought of anything else I could always ask her later. When I came back, we chatted about the weather while I drank my tea.

"You have any more questions, Beth?" Marge said when I'd finished. She really was making it easy for me, which was nice.

"Just a few," I said with an apologetic smile.

She waited.

"Did he ask you for any money recently?"

Marge smiled with satisfaction. "Nope," she said. "He never once asked me for any money."

I was afraid to ask the next question, but I really wanted to know.

"What did his apartment look like on Saturday?" I said.

"Did it look like someone had broken in, or like they'd been looking for something or anything like that?"

Marge took a deep breath and blew it out. "I don't know," she said. "Everything looked normal as far as I remember, but to tell you the truth, Beth, a cyclone could've gone through that place and I mightn't have noticed it. I just wasn't thinking about that."

I nodded, feeling stupid for asking in the first place. I got up and put on my coat.

"Oh, I almost forgot," I said. "Could you give me the name of his cardiologist?"

She wrinkled her brow.

"I want to ask him how Dave might have been given the overdose."

Marge winced slightly, and sighed. She scribbled the cardiologist's name on a napkin and handed it to me. "I'll ask him to talk to you," she said. "I don't think he'll give you any trouble."

"Thanks, Marge," I said, and squeezed her hand.

"Thank you, Beth. Will we see you tomorrow?"

I nodded.

I was tired, despite all the tea. As soon as I got home, I put the car in the garage and went to bed. There was a message on my machine but I didn't even bother to listen to it.

Chapter Three

The next day was Tuesday, December twenty-second, the day of the wake. I wasn't looking forward to that, although I'll have to admit I was looking forward to meeting Jake and Laura. Who would know more about his everyday life than his roommate and his girlfriend? I expected I'd learn a lot from them, assuming they were willing to talk to me.

I got up at seven so I'd have time to eat breakfast before the temp arrived, and I put on a pot of coffee for Emily, who showed up at eight-fifteen.

She looked kind of tired, but just as beautiful as ever. You should see her, she really is gorgeous. She's five-seven, without an ounce of fat on her body. Her eyes are probably her best feature, although it's hard to choose. They're sort of an amber hazel—almost gold, like a cat's—and she has really dark lashes and eyebrows. Her hair's dark brown, too. It's all one length and comes to about the top of her shoulders and it's that really shiny, glossy kind of hair that picks up and reflects every light. And her skin is flawless. It's funny, though. I don't think she's even aware of what she looks like. She's never given any indication of it. Either that or she just takes it for granted.

She took a mug from the cupboard, poured herself some coffee, and plopped down on a chair, her legs extended halfway across the room. Sometimes I wonder what it'd be like to be so tall. Where do you put all those appendages? Don't they just get in the way?

"Late night?" I said with a tentative smile.

She rolled her eyes and shook her head.

"You guys ought to argue during the daytime," I said. "At least you'd get some sleep."

She pressed her lips together and hesitated a moment before responding. "We do that, too," she said with a slight quaver in her voice.

I gave her a sympathetic look, but said nothing. I really don't know what to say when she gets that way. Usually, I just listen when she's in the mood to talk, and she knows I care. I don't know what else to do. I can't come up with any solutions. In the male-female relationship department, I'm at a total loss. No matter how many I have, I never seem to learn a thing. It's more like I'm just perfecting my mistakes.

"You want to talk about it?" I said.

Emily pressed her lips together again and shook her head. "Not now," she said.

I got up, poured myself a cup of coffee, and sat down again. "Where's the temp?" I said. "She was supposed to be here at eight-thirty."

"You can go if you want," Emily said. "I'll take care of her when she gets here."

"Okay," I said. "Thanks."

I really did want to get going. I had to get the research done and it would take me a while, but I didn't want to be late for the wake. Not only was it important to Janice and Marge, but I didn't want to miss Laura or Jake. As it turned out, the night proved to be rather revealing, but not in a way I'd expected.

I went into the library to check my messages before I left and to leave instructions for the typist. My message light was blinking. I reversed the tape and played it back.

"Oh, great," I said. "The temp's not coming until ten."

"Want me to slap her around when she gets here?" Emily said.

I laughed. "No, thanks," I said. "I'll do it myself when I get home."

I wrote out the instructions, told Emily to help herself to anything edible she could find (same for the temp if she ever worked up an appetite), and headed for Marquette.

The sky was overcast, gray, dingy, and depressing. The

roads had been salted, so driving wasn't a problem, but the temperature had dropped to twenty below with a windchill of negative forty. Lovely.

The closest parking space I could find was three blocks from the law library. I grabbed my briefcase, wrapped my scarf around my face, pulled my hat down to my eyebrows, and ran, making sure to sidestep any slick-looking ice patches. By the time I reached the building, my chest felt like someone had plunged two knives in my lungs, my hands and feet were throbbing with pain, and I had ice on my eyelashes. Gosh, I love winter. It's so exhilarating.

I went downstairs for a cup of hot tea to warm myself up. There's a lunchroom in the law school basement across the hall from the student lockers, with soda, coffee, and junk food machines in a little alcove. I peeked in the lunchroom but no one was there. I bought a cup of tea for a quarter and took it upstairs, hoping I could sneak it in.

I signed in, tea unnoticed (it's amazing how you retain certain skills even after years of nonuse), and went down to the Wisconsin Room. The place was full of students, which I hadn't expected, but then I remembered it was the second week of law school exams. (I had one on Christmas Eve, one year.) I found a small spot at the end of one of the tables, sat down, and went right to work.

At one, I was hungry, so I headed for the lunchroom again. I wasn't really in the mood for junk food but I wasn't about to walk anywhere in that cold. I settled for a package of cheese crackers with peanut butter and another cup of tea.

This time the lunchroom was packed. It was a weird feeling not knowing anyone. I felt kind of lonely and envious. I had actually liked law school—a lot. I like school generally. If somebody had been willing to pay me to do it I think I would have gone on forever. Oh, well. The crackers were gone and I was still hungry. I had an ice cream sandwich and another cup of tea, and went back upstairs.

By three o'clock, I'd finished my research. I didn't have to be at the wake until seven so I had just enough time to squeeze

in a little Christmas shopping. Except for the sweater I'd knit-
ted for my dad, I hadn't even started.

Milwaukee's downtown shopping district was converted to an
indoor mall in the early eighties. The mall is on Wisconsin
Avenue but they named it the Grand Avenue Mall because
Wisconsin Avenue was called Grand Avenue way back when.
It's three blocks long, starting with Marshall Field's on Plan-
kinton (which is the equivalent of First Street and immediately
west of the Milwaukee River) and ending at Boston Store on
Fourth.

It's pretty neat. They attached the old Plankinton Arcade,
which was built in the early nineteen-hundreds, to the already
freestanding department stores, and filled in the gaps with new
retail space. I like the Plankinton Arcade part the best (it's
right behind where Big Boy's used to be). It looks like a
European marketplace.

The mall was built as a part of a larger plan to revitalize
the downtown area. They also cleaned up the Milwaukee
River and built condos along the edge. Each one comes with
its own marina slip. The Third Ward (otherwise known as the
warehouse district) was dramatically refurbished. They even
turned some of the old warehouses into apartments. And some
of the new skyscrapers are fantastic (like the 100 East Building on Wisconsin Avenue, for instance).

I parked in the mall parking structure, went in at the second
level, and headed for Marshall Field's. I always go there first.
It used to be Gimbel's, which was my favorite store, but they
went out of business. I stopped at one of the carts and bought
honey and glycerine soaps and moisturizers for Emily, Janice,
and Marge, and Mrs. Gunther and her sister, Erma. I bought
gardenia for my mom and my sister, Ann.

I still wanted something else for my mother and my sister.
I looked through every department at Marshall Field's and
finally found something for my mom near the cosmetics—a
little comb in a cloisonné case and a matching compact. She
loves that sort of thing. I went to the scarf department next,

and bought a brown paisley silk scarf for Mom and a powder-blue silk for Ann.

I went out of the mall, then, and ran across the bridge to Schwartz's Bookshop (my favorite bookstore, considered by many to be the best in the city—it has four branches now) to pick up some books my dad had requested.

Time to go home. I still had two more days before Christmas Eve and I didn't want to finish my shopping all at once. It's one of my favorite parts of the holiday. I went back to the mall, bought a fancy chocolate cake with mocha buttercream frosting, finely chopped walnuts, and chocolate shavings (now how could I pass that up?), and went home.

It was five o'clock. I NordicTracked for twenty minutes, took a shower, dried my hair, and put on a little makeup. Then I searched through my closet. I do own a black dress, but if I'd worn it there'd have been two people at the wake who looked dead. Who am I to steal the limelight? I settled on navy blue instead. I'd still look a little pale, but at least I'd look alive.

I went downstairs, made myself some coleslaw, drank a glass of skim milk, and had a banana. After ingesting all those nutrients I figured I was entitled to a piece of cake. I made a cup of tea to go with it and then had to get going.

The air was still frigid, but the wind had died down considerably. I took I-94 to Hawley Road and then drove down Sixtieth to Lincoln Avenue. Schaff Funeral Home is on the northeast corner of Sixtieth and Lincoln, in the city of West Allis, kitty-corner from St. Rita's Church, where the funeral would be held the next day. When I'm not there for a funeral or a wake, I'm usually glad for an excuse to be in West Allis. I grew up there, and still enjoy going back, just for old times' sake. We moved to Wauwatosa when I was twelve and I liked it there a lot, but I always missed West Allis. I used to fall asleep at night to the sound of a factory (we had a million of them back then), and every morning, around two A.M., I'd hear a train rumble by. It was so darned quiet in Wauwatosa. I couldn't sleep.

It was ten to seven when I arrived at the funeral home, and

the lot was overflowing. I found the room for David Grezinski, walked in, and took my time about signing the guest register. I already had a sick feeling in my stomach. I really hate this sort of thing. The room was full, with everyone speaking in hushed tones and milling about with somber looks on their faces. It was so depressing.

I looked around for Janice and Marge and finally spotted them on the other side of the room. The casket was off to the far right but I averted my eyes, not wanting to look at him. I'd never seen Dave alive, and I wasn't ready yet to see him dead.

When I approached, Marge was talking to a man in a gray suit, who held both her hands as they spoke. Janice was clutching the hand of a woman who stood next to her. The woman appeared to be in her mid-fifties, with brown hair streaked with gray, and a plump, matronly sort of physique. She wore a purple crepe shirtdress with a big brooch on one side.

"Beth," Janice said, and she reached for my hand. Her face was blotchy and her eyes swollen. I gave her a big hug and smiled a hello to Marge and the other woman. Janice introduced the woman as her Aunt Mary and told her I was her best friend. When she said that, I started to cry. I don't know why, I just couldn't help it.

"Why don't you two girls sit down," her Aunt Mary said, "and I'll see if I can rustle you up some coffee."

I smiled. "Thanks," I said. "That would be great."

Another man was talking to Marge then, so I walked with Janice to some folding chairs that were lined up against the walls. Aunt Mary came back a few minutes later with two black coffees in Styrofoam cups.

The heat of the coffee was comforting, and we sat and sipped it for a while, without talking. I looked over at Marge. The man she'd been talking to was gone and had been replaced by a couple about Marge's age. The woman hugged and kissed Marge and the man squeezed her hand. There were two older women talking to Aunt Mary.

"How's your mom doing?" I said.

"I don't know," Janice said with a sigh. "Not too good, I guess. I think it's finally starting to sink in."

I nodded and looked over at Marge again. She was talking to someone else now and her face had the same look I'd seen when I came in. Like all the life had gone out of her, if you'll excuse the expression.

I started checking out the guests, playing a little game with myself. Does she look like an Ethel or a Blanche? What does he do for a living? Does that woman have homicidal tendencies? Is that guy a closet killer?

A group of students stood off to one side. Every one of them looked ill at ease. I wondered if Jake or Laura were among them, but I didn't want to leave Janice right then to find out.

"Is your Aunt Mary your mom's sister?" I asked.

Janice smiled. "Yeah, she's my favorite aunt."

I smiled, too. "She seems really nice," I said.

Our coffee was gone and we just sat there for a while, surveying the crowd. Then Janice let out a big sigh. "Maybe I should go help Mom," she said. But she didn't budge.

"Come on," I said. "I'll go with you."

We stood with Marge for another thirty minutes, while neighbors and friends, some students, Emily and Phil, Mrs. Gunther, and even one of Dave's grade school teachers came over and offered their condolences. I'd asked Janice earlier to point out Jake when she saw him, but she never did. The next forty minutes were spent in organized prayer and a short eulogy, and then it was over.

On their way out, guests lined up to sprinkle holy water on the body and offer a personal prayer. I waited until they were gone, and then forced myself to kneel before the casket as everyone else had done.

I really don't like looking at dead people. It makes me shudder. I keep thinking I see them breathing. I'd never even seen Dave before. I stared at him for as long as I could stand it, trying to memorize his face, trying to imagine what he looked like alive.

I said good-bye, then, to Marge, Janice, and Aunt Mary. Before I left, I looked over the guest list.

No Jake Grossman. And no Laura.

Now that was very strange. It didn't look like Dave's father had shown up either. I wondered if he knew, or if he'd even care. I noticed Dave's cardiologist and his employer had been there, though, and I thought that was nice.

I glanced back as I was about to walk out the door. Marge stood where she had been all evening, but her eyes were focused now on the casket across the room. Janice was holding her by the arm, trying to coax her over to her boy, but Marge was pulling back, shaking her head. I turned away and burst into tears.

At nine fifty-five, I put the car away and hung up my coat. I sat for a long time at the kitchen table with the lights out, and looked out the window. There was nothing out there but inky darkness. No stars and no moon. Even the wind was gone.

I awoke far earlier than I'd intended the next morning, and lay in bed for quite a while, just thinking. It was the day of the funeral. Jake and Laura would *have* to show up for that. At six-thirty, I got up, showered, and dressed. This time, I put on one of the suits I used to wear to court—they work equally well for funerals. I had time enough for a banana and a glass of orange juice, and I made a cup of instant coffee to drink in the car.

The weather really wasn't too bad. It was sunny, and quite cold, but there was very little wind. I took the same route I'd taken the night before and arrived at the church a few minutes before eight.

It had been years since I'd been inside St. Rita's, and it revived a lot of memories. The building is very modern in design, with the roof slanting in all different directions, and enormous stained-glass windows everywhere. It looks the most beautiful when the light filters through, as it did that day. I was married in that church once—the first time. My second husband's funeral was held there. He died three years after we were married. That was ten years ago, December fifteenth.

The service seemed to last forever. As is the custom at masses for the dead, the priest wore black and there wasn't any singing. The altar boys carried incense, swinging the censers above the casket. I tried my best not to listen to the eulogy, willing myself not to cry, but it didn't work. By the time it was over, I felt like I'd eaten hot embers for breakfast instead of fruit.

The burial was worse. I saw Marge cry for the first time, great gulping sobs that shook her whole body. Even Emily had tears in her eyes. After that, we had the traditional after-funeral get-together at Aunt Mary's house, everyone drinking and eating, laughing and joking, talking about everything but Dave and his death. You know, some of the best parties I've been to were after funerals. Now, why is that?

Aunt Mary lives in West Allis, on Fifty-fourth Street, just off of Lincoln Avenue—very close, I realized later, to where Jeffrey Dahmer's grandmother lived until shortly after he was apprehended. Can you imagine? What a hideous thought. Janice could have played with a serial killer when she went to visit her aunt.

Aunt Mary's house is quite common for the area—slate siding, a front porch with steps, stained-oak woodwork throughout, including built-in china cabinets in the dining room, bookcases in the living room, and a pair of stained-glass piano windows. It's a lot like the house I grew up in, except we didn't have the woodwork.

Aunt Mary had a buffet laid out on the dining room table, with hot ham and rolls, two kinds of potato salad, raw beef and onions (this is something Milwaukeeans actually eat, on purpose, and consider some sort of delicacy), coffee, and three kinds of cake. There was also some kind of casserole with potato chips on top, and another made with hot dogs and macaroni and cheese. Yum.

I wasn't hungry just then, so I went to the other table, which was loaded with beer and liquor being served by a neighbor named Sam. I asked for white wine, and he gave me a full twelve ounces in a plastic cup—a little more than I had in mind, but what the heck. It made me shudder every time I took a sip but I was grateful for the numbing effect that went with it.

I looked around the room, feeling slightly uncomfortable, not really knowing what to do with myself. I've always been shy, especially in crowds of people I've never met (even in crowds of people I know, for that matter). I caught sight of Janice and Marge, but both were on the living room couch with an elderly woman between them. The woman must have been ninety years old, so frail she looked like she'd simply blow away in a strong wind. I wandered around, looking for Emily and Phil, but I didn't see them. I knew Mrs. Gunther wasn't there. She'd gone back to the house to get a start on her cleaning.

Laura and Jake! I'd forgotten all about them. I could talk to Laura and Jake. I had no intention of actually discussing the murder right then, but I could introduce myself, give them my number, and ask them to call me. I searched carefully through the entire group, but I couldn't even find anyone who looked under thirty.

Could they both have missed his funeral *and* the wake? It didn't make sense. They had to have been there. They'd probably just neglected to sign the guest register. I knew that neither Janice nor Marge would know Laura, but they'd both recognize Jake. Maybe Janice had just forgotten to mention it. I'd have to ask both of them if they'd seen him.

I'd finished my wine, and it was doing horrible things to my stomach. I felt like I had a little rodent in there, gnawing away at my insides, trying to get out. I know that sounds gross, but that's exactly what it felt like. I decided to have a ham sandwich. At least it would give the varmint something else to chew on.

I was putting some ham on a roll when I heard someone call my name. ''Yes?'' I said as I turned around.

I recognized the man from the funeral home. I'd seen him talking to Marge but we hadn't been introduced. He was fifty, maybe fifty-five, with coarse straight hair a mixture of char-

coal and lighter gray, small, dark-brown eyes, very close together, and bushy gray eyebrows almost meeting in the center.
His nose was large, somewhat swollen and discolored, and his
physique was sort of squishy. He was tall but carried himself
like someone who wished he were shorter—unusual in a man,
I thought. He had a drink in his hand, something like brandy
or Scotch on the rocks, and a thin layer of sweat covered his
brow and upper lip. Not my type. How about yours?

"Ms. Hartley?" he said, extending a clammy hand. "I'm
Dr. King, Dave's cardiologist."

I was surprised, and I think I showed it. I know it's stupid,
but I still expect doctors to look healthy. Nurses, too. Half the
nurses I know, and a good many of the doctors, actually
smoke cigarettes. What's the matter with these people?

"Oh, hello," I said. "I'm very glad to meet you."

"I understand you want to talk to me about Dave," he said.

"Yes, if you don't mind."

"I've already discussed it with his mother," he said. "I'd
be happy to oblige. If you'll call my office first thing Monday
morning I'll instruct my nurse to set aside some time for you.
Just let her know how much you'll need."

"Thank you," I said, and shook his hand again. "I'm sure
half an hour will be plenty."

"Very good, then. I'll look forward to seeing you."

I spotted Janice walking toward me after he left, and I
grinned. "Hey, that was Dr. King, Dave's cardiologist," I
said. "I'm going to talk to him on Monday."

Janice smiled slightly but said nothing.

"How are you doing?" I said.

"Okay," she said. "I'm so glad it's over, though, you
know?"

I nodded, trying to smile with more certainty than I felt. In
my experience, it's a whole lot worse *after* the funeral. When
everyone's gone home, and you're all alone in the house,
that's when you really start to feel the separation. Some of the
most difficult times occur months later, when something happens and your first impulse is to share it with the person, and
then you realize you'd momentarily forgotten he was dead.

That's an awful feeling. I really think those are the worst moments of all.

"Hey, I want to ask you something," I said. "Did you see Jake at either the wake or the funeral?"

Janice gave me a sharp look and wrinkled her brow. "No, I didn't," she said. "But I suppose I could have missed him."

I didn't think so, but I didn't say it. If he had been there, why hadn't he said something to Janice and Marge?

"How about Laura?" I said. "Did she come up and introduce herself?"

"No," Janice said, looking a little perplexed. "Hold on a minute, I'll ask Mom."

Janice came back a few minutes later and said Marge hadn't spoken with either of them, either, and hadn't seen Jake.

I stared off into space for a while, running the information through my head. Both his roommate and his girlfriend failed to show up for his funeral. One would have been weird enough, but both of them? What did they do, run off together? I had a sudden vision of Jake and Laura in some island paradise, lounging in the sun and sipping drinks from coconut shells with little umbrellas poking out. Jake was wearing a Hawaiian shirt and one of those big straw hats with the frayed edges. Laura was in a bikini and she looked fabulous. Well, I'd like to see how good she looks when she's forty-two.

"What are you thinking about?" Janice said, and I gave a little jump.

"Oh, nothing," I said. "I was just wondering where Jake and Laura are."

The look on Janice's face said she didn't really care.

Almost everyone was gone now, including the old woman. I stayed a while longer, said my good-byes, and went home. I had some phone calls to make. I wouldn't be able to track down Laura just yet but I had a good idea how to find Jake.

Chapter Four

It was almost two when I got home. I changed into jeans and a sweatshirt, made myself a cup of tea, and sat at the kitchen table. I had work to do and I knew I should be doing it, but Jake and Laura were really bugging me. After I finished my tea, I picked up the kitchen phone, dialed information, and asked for the number for Jake or Jacob Grossman in Cedarburg, thinking Jake might've been named after his father. No such luck.

"How about J. Grossman?" I said.

"No, ma'am, I'm sorry."

"Okay," I said. "Can you just give me all the Grossmans you have?"

There were seven in all, and I started dialing. The fourth number was the one I was looking for.

A woman answered, identifying herself as Ann Grossman. After learning she was Jake's mother, I introduced myself and told her about Dave's death.

She didn't say anything.

"Mrs. Grossman?" I said.

"I'm sorry," she said, sounding distracted. "I already knew about that. The police were here looking for Jake."

I wasn't sure how to phrase the next question, so I settled for "Did he turn up yet?", and immediately regretted it.

"I . . . uh, no," she said. "But . . ."

"When was the last time you talked to him?" I said.

She hesitated for a moment. "Can I ask what your involvement is in all this?" she said in a snippy voice.

"I'm sorry," I said. "I guess I should have explained that

41

to you. I'm a friend of Dave's sister, Janice, and she believes Dave was murdered. She asked me to help her find out what happened to him and I was just hoping Jake would know something. We'd expected to see him at the funeral but he wasn't there.''

I could hear her catch her breath and then she was silent.

''Mrs. Grossman?'' I said.

''The police said it was a suicide,'' she said in a voice that sounded almost frantic.

''Well, it was made to look like a suicide,'' I said, feeling a little confused by her reaction. ''The police may very well believe it. Mrs. Grossman, did you know Dave?''

''No,'' she said. ''I'm sorry, I have to go now. I have to find Jake.'' And she hung up—just like that.

I thought about it for a few minutes and decided to call her back. From the way she'd sounded, I figured she must be worried that something had also happened to Jake, now that she knew Dave might have been murdered.

She answered on the first ring.

''Mrs. Grossman, please don't hang up. It's me again.''

She made a sound indicating annoyance but stayed on the line. I asked her if she'd agree to let me come to see her so I could help her come up with a way to find Jake. She hesitated, but said okay. After getting directions, I grabbed my jacket and purse and ran out the door.

Cedarburg's about twenty miles north of Milwaukee and it would take me at least thirty minutes to get there, maybe another ten to find her house. I'd been to Cedarburg many times, but the address she gave me was unfamiliar.

The traffic on I-43 was reasonably light, and the sky at least partly sunny. It was a long time since I'd driven that way. My Aunt Sarah and I used to shop there all the time but I hadn't been back since her death. I guess I was afraid it would revive too many memories.

Cedarburg's a beautiful little place with a quaint downtown and a lot of antique shops. Aunt Sarah and I picked up quite a few gems on those shopping trips, mostly walnut and mahogany. She left the furnishings as well as the house to me. The pieces we bought together are my favorites.

Mrs. Grossman's directions were surprisingly good, given her state of mind when she gave them to me. The house was at the end of a cul-de-sac lined with ash and maple trees. The lots were big, probably half an acre or more, and the houses were large and ostentatious—a lot of those French country manor things that look so out of place in a subdivision. No sidewalks, either. And enormous front yards no one ever uses. Personally, I'd rather have my land in the back and on the sides, and have sidewalks so I don't have to walk in the street.

The Grossman residence was an imposing beige Tudor with dark brown trim and a deep red door. A brick walkway led from the street to the front steps, which were constructed of the same brown and beige brick. To the right of the doorway, three large oaks were arranged in a conversational grouping for trees. The Christmas decorations were simple but elegant, large wreaths with gold bows and tiny white lights.

I lifted the brass door knocker and rapped twice. The wind was starting to pick up again and the sky was overcast now, with some pretty ominous-looking clouds in the distance. I pulled my collar up and jumped up and down a few times to keep warm. I was on the "up" side of a jump when she opened the door. I smiled and her brows lifted just a teensy bit.

Mrs. Grossman wasn't far from what I'd expected in terms of appearance. She looked to be in her late forties, maybe early fifties. Very thin, about five-six or -seven. She was dressed in beige tailored slacks (linen, I think) and a perfectly coordinated sweater. Gold earrings, gold bangle bracelet, gold rings on each hand. Her hair was blond with carefully placed streaks, worn short in a style I've seen on a hundred women her age. They were blonds, too, come to think of it. Maybe that's part of the style.

Her nails looked professionally done, painted a deep shade of rose. Her features were regular but not remarkable. Thin lips, average nose, blue eyes. The only thing wrong with the picture she presented was her makeup. What little she was wearing was smudged and on the wrong parts of her face.

She glanced nervously over my head, peered outside, and pulled me in and shut the door before I'd even identified myself.

"I'm Beth Hartley," I said, smiling again.

She looked a little startled, and for a moment I thought she'd mistaken me for somebody else. "Yes . . . I mean . . . I'm sorry," she said, shaking her head. "You'll have to forgive me. I don't know where my head is. Please come in. May I call you Beth?"

"Oh, sure," I said.

"Please call me Ann."

She led me through a foyer tiled in large black and white squares like a big chessboard. I've always wanted a floor like that. If you got enough people together you could play chess on it just like in *Alice in Wonderland.* Wouldn't that be fun? The woodwork and staircase (off to the right and straight ahead) were painted a gleaming white, the walls papered in a gold-and-white fleur-de-lis print. The entryway to the living room was on the left.

The woodwork there was also white, the carpet a deep shade of gold. Two white brocade couches were arranged in the center of the room, facing each other, with a large square oak table between them. Matching wing chairs, upholstered in a white, gold, and green stripe, faced the fireplace on the wall opposite the doorway. The artwork was of a modern sort, and some of it looked original. To my left, in front of the window, was a gorgeous Steinway grand piano. (I've wanted one of those since I was five, but I've always felt I didn't play well enough to deserve one.)

Mrs. Grossman offered me a seat on one of the couches and sat down herself on the other.

"I love your piano," I said. "Do you play?"

She looked surprised, as if she'd forgotten it was there. "Oh, no," she said. "None of us can really play."

I nodded.

"I'm sorry," she said. "Would you like coffee? Or soda? I have Diet Coke and Fresca."

I smiled, not really wanting anything but afraid I'd offend her if I turned it down. "Coffee would be great," I said.

She smiled, looking almost grateful, and said she'd be right back. She returned a few minutes later with a tray, holding two mugs of coffee, a pitcher of what looked like skim milk, artificial sweetener, and a plate of oatmeal cookies.

"These are fat-free," she said in a conspiratorial voice, "but they're really good."

I grinned and took one, wondering why in the world she felt she needed to diet. She had no excess fat anywhere on her body, from what I could see.

She gave me a sheepish smile, as if she'd read my mind. "I lost forty-three pounds in the last year and I'm terrified I'll gain it back," she said. "Divorce," she added with a rueful look. "Got myself a new hairdo, too." She moved her head around so I could inspect it.

"Well, I'm sorry about the divorce," I said, "but you look great. You really do. And the hairdo's perfect on you."

"Thanks," she said with a wide grin. "I appreciate your coming all the way out here. I'm sorry if I seemed rude on the phone."

"No, you didn't," I said. "That was my fault. I should've explained myself before I started firing questions at you."

"Do you have any experience at this sort of thing? Are you a private investigator?"

"No," I said, laughing. "I have no experience at all. But Janice is convinced the police will never pursue a murder theory so she begged me to help her and I just couldn't say no. She seemed so desperate."

She nodded. "I understand."

"You know, I realize you're worried something might've happened to Jake," I said, "but I don't think there's any reason to believe that's true."

Mrs. Grossman pressed her lips together and tears suddenly filled her eyes. "I'm sorry," she said, and took a tissue from her pocket.

"That's all right," I said. "I'm not sure how to say this without upsetting you even more, but I think if Jake had been killed, too, he'd have been found with Dave. It seems so unlikely that he'd be killed somewhere else or that they'd move his body but not Dave's. You know what I mean?"

She looked at me, tears still in her eyes, but there was a smile poking through. "You really think so?" she said, sniffling.

"Yes, I really do."

Mrs. Grossman took a deep breath and closed her eyes, then let it out and leaned her head back against the couch. "I can't see why he wouldn't have gone to the funeral, though," she said. "Where would he go for so long a time? He must not know about it. I'm sure he would've been there if he did."

I nodded, giving her a look that feigned agreement.

"When was the last time you talked to him?" I said.

"Thanksgiving. He was here for the day and went back to his apartment the day after."

"And you haven't talked to him since?"

"No," she said, shaking her head. "But that isn't unusual. I often don't hear from him for weeks at a time. He has his own life. You know how it is."

"I hate to ask this, but do you know if he talks to his father?"

"No," she said. "George hasn't spent a moment of time with Jake since the divorce. Of course, he never spent any time with him before the divorce, so I suppose that shouldn't surprise me."

I gave her a sympathetic smile, not really knowing how to respond to that. "How about friends?" I said. "Does he have anyone in the neighborhood he usually sees?"

"There's Bob Sheridan down the street."

"Do you know if he talked to him at Thanksgiving?"

Mrs. Grossman sat up a bit straighter. "Yes," she said. "He did. He went over to the house before he left on Friday. He must've been there an hour or more."

I raised my eyebrows and gave her a little smile. "It might be worth calling him," I said.

"Yes, just a minute, I'll get the number." Mrs. Grossman left the room, returned with an address book opened to the number, and handed it to me. "Here it is," she said.

"Do you want me to call him?"

She gave me a plaintive look with a little sheepishness mixed in. "Would you?" she said.

"Sure. Where's your phone?"

She led me through a dining room with an enormous pale oak table that probably could have seated twelve comfortably, and a matching sideboard and china cabinet. The carpet was the same deep gold as in the living room, the walls papered in a gold, green, and white stripe pattern that looked a lot like the wing chairs in front of the fireplace. The drapes were green brocade with balled fringe. The table was set for eight, with china, silver, a full set of crystal, and cloth napkins.

"Are you expecting company tonight?" I asked, afraid I'd interrupted her preparations.

"Oh, no," Mrs. Grossman said. "I always keep it set."

I followed her into the next room, which looked like a small den. The floors were hardwood, with a deep red Oriental rug on top. Bookcases covered three of the walls and an oak roll-top desk was pushed against the fourth. The phone was on the desk.

I punched in the number and a woman answered on the fifth ring. I gave her my name, told her I was a friend of Jake, and asked for Bob. When she said she'd get him, I smiled at Mrs. Grossman and nodded.

A minute went by. Two minutes. When Bob finally picked up the phone he sounded as if I'd roused him out of bed.

"Hullo?" he said.

"Bob?"

"Yeah, this is Bob. Who's this?"

I introduced myself and said Jake's mother and I were looking for Jake, but I didn't explain why.

"Uh . . . well, what do you want him for?" he said.

I decided I'd better give Bob the whole story if I wanted to get any information out of him. I told him how Dave had died, that we suspected he'd been murdered, that Jake hadn't been at the funeral, that his mother didn't know where he was, that she was worried something had happened to him in addition to Dave, and that we desperately needed his help in locating Jake.

He was wide awake now, listening to every word, interrupting me at appropriate junctures with phrases such as ''Are you putting me on?'' and ''Whoa, this is some heavy stuff, man.'' I kept smirking, and Mrs. Grossman was giving me funny looks.

''Do you have any idea where he is?'' I said when I'd finished.

Now he was silent.

''Please,'' I said. ''This is really important. He's not in any trouble, if that's what you're worried about.''

Bob hesitated for a moment and then I heard him sigh. ''He said something about hitting Green Bay before he went home.''

''Green Bay?'' I said. ''Why was he going there?''

Mrs. Grossman wrinkled her brow at me and I shrugged.

''He went to play blackjack,'' Bob said. ''There's a casino there. It's legal, you know.''

''I know,'' I said. ''But why didn't he just go to the Milwaukee casino?''

''I don't know,'' Bob said. ''Maybe he was tired of it. What difference does it make?''

''It doesn't,'' I said, starting to feel defensive. ''I was just asking. Did he tell you how long he was going to be in Green Bay?''

''No, but he wouldn't have stayed this long. That was right after Thanksgiving.''

''You haven't talked to him since then?''

''Nope,'' Bob said.

''You wouldn't have any idea where else he might've gone, would you?''

''Sorry,'' he said. ''It's not my week to watch him.'' Boy, do I hate it when people say that.

''Okay,'' I said. ''Well, thanks, Bob. If you do hear from him, would you let his mom know?''

"Sure thing," Bob said. Yeah, I just bet he would.

I looked at Mrs. Grossman after I hung up. "Well, he says Jake went to Green Bay to some casino to play blackjack but that was right after Thanksgiving. He has no idea where he is now."

Mrs. Grossman shook her head. "He must be mistaken," she said. "Jake doesn't play blackjack."

I shrugged. "Maybe it was his first time."

Mrs. Grossman looked at me with a combination of worry and irritation.

We walked back to the living room and sat down. "Well," I said. "Maybe we should try to think of someone else he might've talked to."

She didn't say anything.

"Does Jake have a job?" I said.

"No. I don't want him working during school. His grades suffer too much."

"Is there anyone else you can think of?"

Mrs. Grossman just shook her head and stared off into space.

"We probably ought to tell the police about Green Bay," I said.

She took a deep breath and pursed her lips.

"It might help them find him," I said. "I can do it for you if you want."

She looked up then and gazed at me for a few moments. "No, I'll do it," she said.

I gave Mrs. Grossman my phone number and asked her to please call me if she heard anything from Jake. She said she would. I said good-bye, told her not to worry too much, and left.

I thought about Jake all the way home. Maybe he had a gambling habit and took off for a casino every chance he got. He could be one of those guys who hangs out for days, not even bothering to take a shower. Maybe he really hadn't heard about Dave's death.

I considered calling the police myself, when I got home,

but I didn't really want them knowing what I was doing—about my investigating and all. I decided to call Emily instead.

"Hi, what's up?" I said.

"Not much, how about you?"

"I went to see Dave's roommate's mom in Cedarburg. He never showed up at the funeral."

"That's weird," Emily said.

"Yeah, I know."

"What'd his mom say?"

"She hasn't even talked to him since Thanksgiving, but some guy he hangs around with says he goes to Green Bay to play blackjack."

"Ooh, a little gambling action, huh? Maybe that's where he is now."

"Yeah, that's what I was thinking. Want to drive up there and see if we can find him?"

"What, are you nuts?" Emily said. "Let the police find him. I can't believe you're actually going through with this, anyway. It's really stupid, you know. You could get yourself in a lot of trouble."

"I'm not going to get in any trouble," I said. "All I did was talk some woman about her kid. What's the big deal?"

"Well, what if the killer finds out you're doing this, then what?"

"Just drop it, okay? What are you doing now?"

"Nothing, why?"

"Want to go to the Downtown Club?"

Emily hesitated. "Tell you what," she said. "I'll meet you in the whirlpool."

I laughed. "Okay, great. What time?"

"Half an hour?"

"Great. I'll see you there."

I ran upstairs, got my swimming suit and workout clothes, drank a glass of orange juice, and got in the car. The Downtown Club is on Van Buren and Juneau so it only takes about ten minutes to get there.

I signed in, put on my workout clothes, and went to the weight room. I jumped rope for fifteen minutes, used a couple of machines, and decided to quit. There wasn't anyone else in the room. I usually dislike exercising in front of other people (especially men!) but it felt kind of eerie being there all alone.

I went back to the locker room and changed into my bathing suit, then peeked around the door to the pool room before I went in. Good. No men. I hate walking past men in my bathing suit.

Emily was in the whirlpool with her eyes closed and her head laid back against the edge. Two young women were in the sauna and an older woman, about fifty-five or sixty, was in the pool, swimming slow laps. Other than that, we had the place to ourselves.

"Hi," I said.

Emily opened her eyes. "Nice suit," she said with a smirk.

"What's wrong with it?" I said in a defensive voice.

"You look like Gidget," she said, and closed her eyes again.

I made a face she didn't see but kept my mouth shut. I'm such a wimp when it comes to stuff like that. I can always think of the perfect comeback two hours later but when someone says something to me (especially Emily), I just stand there like a dummy.

"Did you go to the house after the funeral?" Emily said when I got in the pool.

"Yeah, it was pretty nice. Dave's girlfriend never showed up either, by the way. Isn't that bizarre?"

"Yeah, it really is. You know, I was thinking," Emily said. "Remember Brian McHenry from grade school?"

"Ha. Brian McHenry. You bet I remember him. Why?"

"He's a homicide detective with the Milwaukee Police Department."

"You're kidding," I said. "How do you know that?"

Emily shrugged. "He went to the police academy with my brother. And," she said, the corners of her mouth turning up just slightly, "I went out with him for a while."

"You went out with him?" I said. "You're kidding. You never told me that. When'd you go out with him?"

"Right before law school, during the summer."

"I can't believe you never told me that. How'd you end up going out with him?"

"Steve and Lynn. They were having him over to dinner all the time when he got divorced and they sort of set me up with him—without telling me ahead of time."

"I'd kill my brother if he ever did that to me."

"Yeah, I almost did," Emily said.

"Well, what was he like? What does he look like now?"

"Really good," Emily said. "He's six-two and he has a really great build. You can tell he works out. And he looks . . . I don't know, really good. He has nice hair and he wears wire-rims. Dresses nicely, too."

I grinned, trying to conjure up an image of our class nerd looking really good when he grew up. He was the smartest kid in our class. He wore glasses with black plastic frames and he wasn't one of the guys the girls drooled over, but I'd always found him appealing. I think it was his intelligence. And he was really nice, too. Kind and considerate.

"How long did you go out with him?" I said.

"Just a couple of months."

"Why'd you stop seeing him?"

"He went back to his wife."

"Ah."

"They were going to try to work things out," Emily said. "It was so stupid. If they were going to work things out, why didn't they do it when they were married?"

I sighed. "So what happened? Did they get married again?"

"No, she took off again."

"Did you go out with him after that?"

"I'd already met Phil by then. I guess I always did have lousy timing."

I frowned at her. "You mean you wish you'd gone back to Brian instead?"

Emily shrugged and made a face that said, "Who knows? Who cares?"

"Phil really loves you, you know. Frankly, the guy worships you. That's not easy to find."

Emily didn't say anything. She didn't open her eyes, either, but I could see her clenching her jaw. In a few moments, she stood up and got out of the whirlpool.

"I'm going for a swim," she said.

I watched her do thirty laps at a pace at least twice that of the poor woman in the lane next to her. Then she got out and wanted to go home.

"Why'd you bring up Brian McHenry?" I asked her when we were getting dressed. "What'd you want to say about him?"

"I just thought you could talk to him about the case, see if he'd tell you anything."

"Hey, that's a thought," I said, "although he probably wouldn't give me any information. It'd be worth a try, though.

"You want to go get something to eat?" I said then.

"No, I'd better not," Emily said. "Phil will be home pretty soon, and I haven't cooked for a while. I was planning to make roast beef and I already took it out of the freezer."

"Okay. Say 'hi' for me."

"Will do. Talk to you later."

I got in my car and sat. I didn't want to go home. I decided to go Christmas shopping again. Tomorrow was Christmas Eve and I wasn't anywhere near through with my gift buying. I took I-94 west, then US-45, and got off on Mayfair Road.

The Mayfair Mall is in Wauwatosa, and it's about what you'd expect. Classy stores, tony decor. It used to have an ice-skating rink in the center, but it's gone now. In its place, during the holidays, is the largest Christmas tree I've ever seen indoors. It's decorated in the best of taste, too. Nothing but little white lights, big red balls, and silver bows. It looks *really* good if you're nearsighted and you don't have your glasses on.

I had a lot of trouble finding a place to park, and was almost ready to turn back, when someone pulled out of a space very near my usual entrance. I parked, ran in, and then slowed down, taking my time to wander around. I can spend hours in a mall, especially near Christmas.

I found gifts for my father and brother and another for my sister, Ann. I went through my mental list. I'd taken care of everyone but my sister's kids, and I could take care of that tomorrow. Well, okay. Then I was done.

It was snowing when I left—big, fat flakes, my favorite kind. I opened my mouth and ate a few. I know you're not supposed to do that but it hasn't killed me yet. My grandmother taught me that important lesson (the flakes fall through polluted air, you know) along with many others. Always wear a hair net when you go out-of-doors (it was never "outside," always "out-of-doors"). Never sit next to a man on a bus. Never chew with your mouth open (I agree with that one), and never wear patent leather shoes with a dress. There were others, but I can't remember them right now. If I do think of any, though, I'll be sure to let you know.

There was already a good two inches on the ground and it was really coming down. The salt, sand, and plowing crews were doing their best but the highway was pretty slick. Most of us slowed down to a creep, but the occasional moron (that's an alternate spelling for "man") would whip by at the posted speed.

When I got home an hour later, I put the car in the garage and went in through the back door so I could take my wet clothes off in the mudroom. (The back door opens to the mudroom, which is right off the kitchen.) On the other side of the mudroom is another door, which opens to the basement. I think it's really handy, but my Aunt Sarah thought it was inconvenient. She actually had my Uncle Bill build a clothes chute from the kitchen to the top of the basement stairs, just so she wouldn't have to go through the mudroom to put her laundry downstairs. It's just a square hole in the wall, with doors on both sides. I never use it myself because I don't like having clothes on my basement steps.

I made myself a cup of tea, and looked through the refrigerator for something to eat. I didn't have much, which isn't unusual since I hate to go grocery shopping. I decided on a frozen pizza. I brought some work into the kitchen and wrote while I waited for the pizza to bake. The flakes were falling even faster now, full and fluffy. I smiled and watched, feeling safe and warm inside my house. I ate my supper, took a cup of hot chocolate into the library (I love hot chocolate when it's snowing), and read for about an hour. At ten, I went upstairs, read a little longer, and turned out the light.

Snuggled under my covers, I thought snowy thoughts and dreamt snowy dreams. White-capped mountain peaks and frosted evergreens. Silent, dark forests, the soft secret sound of snow falling in the night, and breezes whispering to the trees.

I woke up with a smile on my face. It was Christmas Eve. I didn't know it then, but that was the day I would learn what had happened to Jake.

Chapter Five

As soon as I opened my eyes, I ran to the window to see how much snow we'd gotten.

A lot. A whole lot. Like a couple of feet? Good grief.

I have a neighbor boy on a sort of retainer to shovel my walk, front and back, whenever it needs it. He was out in front of my house, just getting started. I opened the window wide enough to stick my head out and got a blast of cold air and snow in the face.

"Hey, Peter. Merry Christmas," I yelled.

Peter stopped shoveling and looked up with a grin. "Hey, how're ya doin'?" he said.

"Great. Come around back when you're through. I have something for you."

He grinned, knowing what it was—a big fat Christmas bonus I give him every year.

The whole neighborhood was full of people shoveling, most with snowblowers rather than shovels, though. I guess I should break down and buy one so Peter won't have to work so hard. I think he enjoys it, though. (Yeah, right, who am I kidding?) The street was already plowed, leaving three-foot banks along each side. I love that. Sometimes I still walk across them when I'm pretty sure nobody's looking.

I made the bed, showered and dressed, and went down to the kitchen. Snow always makes me hungry, and I was starving. I turned on my kitchen radio, made a pot of tea, and baked some blueberry muffins. I wasn't due at my parents' house until noon and it was only nine so I had plenty of time. I had

56

a bit of shopping to do before I went but I didn't think it would take too long.

At ten-fifteen, Peter knocked at the door and I asked him in for a cup of hot chocolate and some muffins. He was thrilled. He looked like a big icicle, poor kid. He's sixteen, a junior in high school, and I love talking to him. He dripped snow all over my kitchen floor, and me, but I didn't care.

At ten-forty-five, I loaded my presents in the car and headed for the expressway. I couldn't wait to get to my parents' house—partly because it was Christmas Eve, of course, but also because I had something I wanted to ask my brother, Mike, about Dave. I'd have to wait until I got a chance to talk to him alone, though. And I'd have to wait for everything, until after I got my shopping done.

I took 894 to Seventy-sixth Street and stopped at Barnes & Noble on my way to the toy store. I buy a lot of books there, even though it's way across town, because I really like the store. It's enormous, the staff is very helpful, and they have a great coffee shop.

Seventy-sixth Street is one of those commercial strips with movie theaters, shopping malls, and every fast-food restaurant in existence. Barnes & Noble is a relatively recent addition. The traffic is often heavy, but today it was heavier than usual. I hadn't expected so many people to be out on Christmas Eve, especially with all the snow.

The parking lot was plowed, the snow pushed over to one end forming a mountain at least ten feet high (we used to make snow forts out of those when we were kids). The book-store was crowded but I was kind of glad. It was more festive that way. I looked around for a while, found some books for Ann's kids, and a couple of mysteries for myself. I stood in a long line, which moved very quickly, paid for the books, and brought them back to the coffee shop.

I love that café. I could sit there for hours. It has a player piano and it was playing jazz renditions of Christmas carols when I came in. I found a table, ordered coffee with cream, and sat down.

An older couple (maybe mid- to late sixties) was sitting at

the table next to mine. The woman had wavy silver hair and she was wearing the most beautiful seafoam-green sweater with a plaid wool skirt, long wool stockings, and short boots. The man had a beard, wore wide-wale corduroy pants, an old cardigan with leather patches on the elbows, and a wool, herringbone-checked hat that looked sort of like a tam with a visor. He was reading a newspaper and she was eating cake. Every once in a while, she'd give him a bite. Every so often, he'd read something to her from the paper. They looked so companionable. I think I'd like to be married at that age, but it'd have to be to the right sort of person. Someone whose company I enjoy. Someone who appreciates my good qualities. My first husband saw all my best qualities as faults. Now, how's that for building your self-esteem?

A few tables over, two college-age kids were playing Scrabble (with a game supplied by the café) and drinking some kind of fancy coffee with that funny milk on top. I hate that stuff. The coffee's always too strong and the milk feels weird. I like regular old-fashioned coffee with regular old-fashioned cream (although whipped cream is awfully good). Ann says I'm just not hip. Oh, well. Her husband, Don, is. He always orders a "double cap." I'm pretty sure that means double cappuccino, but I've never had the nerve to ask. I guess I'd know if I were hip, huh? Heck, if I were hip, I wouldn't even care. I'd just order the stuff, drink it, and pretend I liked it even if it made me gag.

Don smokes a pipe, too, with some expensive tobacco he never shuts up about. You should see this guy. He's about five-ten, maybe thirty pounds overweight, light brown hair, and a really scraggly beard. He wears a tweed sportcoat and jeans all the time, even in summer, and he says things like, "It's very sort of . . ." and "One finds that . . ." Talk about things that make you gag.

I sipped my coffee and read the back covers of my mysteries. After a second cup, I decided I'd better get going. I still had the kids' toys to buy and I had to pick up a mincemeat pie I'd ordered from Baker's Square for my dad. How anyone can eat a pie made of suet is beyond me, but Dad loves it so I get him one every year.

The toy store I was so sure was close by was no longer there. Luckily, Southridge Shopping Center is just down the street so I went there to Kay-Bee Toys. I found a purportedly safe chemistry set for ten-year-old Don, a set of K'NEX for seven-year-old Kristin, and Tinkertoys for five-year-old Katy. It's so much easier now that they're older. I have the hardest time finding toys for toddlers. It's that ubiquitous "not suitable for children under three" that causes all the problems.

Baker's Square is also on Seventy-sixth Street, on the same side of the street as Southridge. I picked up the animal fat pie, put it in the trunk, and drove down Seventy-sixth to Bluemound, then took Bluemound to Eighty-fourth. My parents' house is on Eighty-fourth Street, a few blocks north of Bluemound. I drove slowly through the neighborhood so I could look at the decorations.

Most of the houses were decorated, but everything was pretty subdued. Tiny white lights. Wreaths with bows. An occasional crèche. Nothing like West Allis, where, in at least one neighborhood, they put on an extravaganza you wouldn't believe.

My mom has something different each year and she makes everything herself. This time it was wreaths of ferns and pinecones with red apples and big red plaid bows. The best on the block, as always. The street is lined with mature deciduous trees, mostly maples and oaks, and all the houses are different. Ours is red brick with dark green shutters (the real thing with wrought-iron hinges) and a dark red door. In the summer, my mother's pink roses form an arch over the door and she has pale pink gardenias in every window box. Blossoming beauty everywhere. I always mean to try something like it at my own house but I've never made the time.

I parked behind Don's Range Rover, gathered up all my stuff, and went inside. The house opens to a foyer with a big hall tree and a small table for mail and keys and such things. The living room has stuccoed walls, painted off-white. The couch and the love seat are a plum-and-cream plaid. There are two wing chairs in a plum-and-navy print on a braided wool rug a few feet from the fireplace. The wood furniture is walnut, bought at secondhand shops or estate sales and refinished by my mom. There's an antique desk against one wall, a large chest against another, and a gateleg table to the left of the love seat. Above and on each side of the fireplace, from floor to ceiling, are bookshelves constructed by my grandfather.

A fire was burning in the fireplace and Dad was using it to roast chestnuts and pop corn for the kids. I gave him a big hug and kiss, and moved the kids a little farther from the fire. I love the ambience of a crackling fire but it does make me nervous. I settled the kids on the rug with the corn my dad had already popped, and went to the kitchen to find my mom.

She was there, with Ann, making cornflake cookies (sounds weird but they're great). The kitchen is small, but nice and homey. The floor is reddish-brown ceramic tile and the wall behind the oven is the same red brick as the outside of the house. The other walls are off-white (stucco again) with a chair rail and oak paneling beneath it. The cabinets are oak, too, and so are the table and chairs. And there's a walk-in pantry.

I kissed Mom and Ann and poured myself a cup of coffee.

"Where's Donny Dear?" I said to Ann.

She shot me a look. "Do you have to call him that?" she said.

"Sorry, I thought it was a term of endearment," I said. She wasn't fooled. I could tell. Oh, well. That's what she gets for marrying him, I guess.

"He's in the library," she said grudgingly.

"How's Janice holding up?" my mom asked.

"Oh, that is so awful what happened to her brother," Ann said. "I just can't believe it."

"Yeah, I know," I said. I told them how I thought both Janice and Marge were faring and that Janice believed Dave had been murdered. I left out the part about her asking me to help her find the killer.

"Oh, my Lord," my mom said.

"Oh, that is so horrible," Ann said.

I agreed, again, and tried to change the subject, but just then Mike walked in and wanted to know what was so horrible. I told him the story then, and added a few details about Dave's career plans, since he'd intended to start a business so much like Mike's. I finally succeeded in changing the subject after that by asking Ann about the kids. We talked about Don, Jr.'s basketball and soccer prowess for the next half-hour, and the murder was forgotten.

The rest of the evening was our typical Christmas Eve. Lasagna, mostoccioli, Italian sausage, and meatballs for supper, a ride after dinner to look at the lights, and then home to open presents Santa Claus conveniently left while we were out.

We put the kids to bed at eight, and played games until almost midnight. When Mike went to the basement to replenish the soda between Risk and Monopoly, I offered to help.

"Let me ask you something," I said when we were out of everyone else's earshot. "If somebody wanted to break into a computer at Marquette to change their grades or something like that, would they need to do it in any particular building or could they just do it from any computer?"

He looked at me with puzzlement and surprise. "What do you want to know that for?" he said.

I told Mike about the bomb scares. "I was just wondering if Dave could've been using them as a ruse to get access to a computer."

"No. He wouldn't have to do that," Mike said. "If anyone could get in those files and change their grades—which they almost certainly couldn't, by the way—they could do it from home if they had a modem."

"Why couldn't they get in?" I said.

"It's encrypted and encoded to death. It'd be almost impossible to figure it out. Some engineering students got in years ago and after that they made it pretty much burglarproof."

I sighed. "Okay, thanks," I said.

"What are you so interested in that for?" Mike said.

"I don't know," I said with a shrug. "He was Janice's brother, that's all."

The drive home was peaceful. Everything was quiet and the sky was full of stars. I put the car away, wished Orion a Merry Christmas, and went inside.

I went into the library to see if I had any messages. There was one. It was Ann Grossman. Jake had been found. He'd come home for Christmas.

Hallelujah, I thought as I scrunched under the covers. Ann Grossman's child was safe.

I slept until ten and then hurried to get dressed. I'd promised my mom I'd be back before noon so I could help with the Christmas Day meal, but I had to call Ann Grossman first. It was a little early, so I had a banana and some toast and made myself a cup of tea. I sorted through Christmas cards until a quarter to eleven and then made the call.

"Ann? This is Beth Hartley," I said when she picked up the phone.

"Beth. Thank you for calling. I wanted you to know Jake is all right and to thank you for all your help," she said. She was so excited and so happy it brought tears to my eyes.

"You're very welcome," I said. "Did the police find him?"

"No," she said. "He just came home. He came home because it was Christmas." From the sound of her voice, it was the best Christmas present she'd ever received.

"I'm so glad," I said. "I know how worried you were."

"Yes, I was," she said. "And thank you again, Beth. Merry Christmas to you and all your family."

When I thanked her and wished her the same, she was about to hang up.

"Ann?" I said. "Would you mind if I talked to Jake for a few minutes?"

She hesitated and then said, "No. No, of course not. I'll go get him. He's already talked to the police, by the way."

A few minutes later, she returned and said Jake would be

right down. When he finally picked up the phone he sounded a little nervous.

"Jake?" I said. "My name is Beth Hartley and I'm a good friend of Dave's sister, Janice."

"Yeah, I know Janice," he said.

"Well, she's asked me to help her prove Dave was murdered and I was hoping you could help me."

"The police are working on that," Jake said.

"I know," I said, "but Janice is afraid they won't take it seriously enough or they'll just abandon it too soon or something."

"Yeah, so what do you want from me?" he said. "I already told everything I know to the police."

"Would you mind telling me, too?"

He grunted in annoyance.

"I know it seems like a waste of time," I said, "but you'll be doing Janice a big favor."

He sighed loudly. "Yeah, okay," he said grudgingly. "But not on the phone. Can you come to my place tomorrow?"

"Sure. What time?"

"Eleven?"

"That'd be great," I said. "Thanks, Jake."

I called Janice next, but there was no answer. I tried Marge and didn't get an answer there, either.

I went to my parents' house, spent the rest of the day eating Christmas cookies and trying to fix broken toys, and was back home by ten. I was still tired from the night before. I made myself a cup of chamomile tea and went up to bed.

The next day was Saturday, December twenty-sixth. I awoke at nine and took my time getting dressed. It had snowed lightly during the night and everything was dusted with a clean white powder. I made apple muffins for breakfast and ate three along with two cups of tea. I called Janice at ten and asked if she wanted to go with me to talk to Jake, but she said no. She didn't want to go into the apartment again. Not just yet, anyway.

"How was your Christmas?" I asked in a cautious voice.

Janice let out a big sigh. "It was miserable," she said. "But we went to Aunt Mary's both days. We always have Christmas at home, so that made it easier."

"Well, that's good," I said. "I'm glad you had somewhere else to go."

Janice sighed again. "We don't know what to do with the presents we bought him," she said, her voice breaking.

"Oh, my gosh," I said. "I know just what you mean."

"What did you do with Eric's?"

"I kept them," I said. "But I put them in a box in the attic where I don't have to see them unless I want to."

Janice didn't say anything for a few moments, but I could hear her sniffling. "Yeah," she said after a bit. "That's a good idea."

"What are you planning to do today?"

"I don't know. Go over to Mom's, I guess." She sounded so hopeless and lost it brought tears to my eyes.

"Are you going to be all right?" I said.

"Yeah, I guess. Will you call me when you get back?"

"Sure," I said.

Jake's apartment is on the east side, just off of Brady, in the old Italian ward. At one time, the neighborhood was populated almost exclusively by Italian-Americans. A lot of them are still there. In the sixties and early seventies, the area became a hippie hangout. Drug paraphernalia shops and other counterculture establishments moved in, and some of the residents moved out. Nearly all of that's gone now. You'd hardly know they'd been there.

Jake's building is a light salmon brick in an art deco style. I found the button for the apartment to the left of the mailboxes and rang. A few moments later, the door clicked and I walked in.

The lobby was sprawling, with brocade-curtained floor-to-ceiling windows, a checkerboard-tiled floor in tan and beige, and a winding staircase with a painted railing and steps covered with worn Oriental carpeting.

I took the stairs to the third floor. Jake's number was 314.

The door to the apartment next to Jake's was wide open, and another, farther down the hall, was slightly ajar. The one next door appeared to be inhabited by a woman, probably elderly, if I could judge by the furnishings. I knocked on Jake's door.

"It's open," I heard.

A young man was standing about eight feet from the doorway, packing items into a box. The box was on a coffee table in front of the couch. He was about five-nine or-ten, of normal weight except for a slight paunch. His black hair was long, about two inches over his ears, and he looked like he was starting a beard. He wore a brown one-pocket T-shirt over faded blue jeans. The jeans had holes all over them.

"You Beth?" he said, not bothering to look up.

"Yes," I said. "I assume you're Jake?"

He didn't respond so I took that as a yes. He went right on with his packing.

The room was large and square, the floor bare wood with most of the varnish peeled off. The couch was to my right, a drab olive green, partially covered by an orange, red, and blue afghan. Across from the couch was a stereo, a CD player, two speakers, a TV, and a VCR. The wall directly across from the door was all windows, but the only view was of a brick wall from the building next door. The plants hanging in the window were yellow and wilted.

"Are you moving?" I asked.

"Yep," he answered, and went right on with what he was doing. He still hadn't taken a peek at me. If he was trying to make me feel uncomfortable, he was doing a darn good job of it.

"I asked Janice if she wanted to come with me," I said, "but she didn't want to see the apartment again. She was the one who found Dave, you know."

Jake tightened his jaw, but said nothing. He'd been packing things in a careful way up to that point, but now he started flinging things, one after the other, into the open box. He just took whatever was closest and pitched it in. When something shattered, he threw the next three items in with particular force, punctuated each time by what I soon learned was his expletive of choice.

He dropped himself onto the couch, and stared out the window with his teeth clenched.

"Would you like me to help you with that?" I said.

"No. Forget it," he muttered.

I sat down on the other end of the couch.

"Nice view," I said.

He turned his head, stared at me in disbelief, and laughed. He shook his head a few times, a smile still on his face.

"Do you want me to come back some other time?" I said.

"No, forget it," he said. "I'm sorry, you want a beer or something?"

"No, thanks," I said, stifling a laugh.

Jake sighed, then sighed again. "So, what'd you want to ask me?" he said.

"Well, quite a few things," I said. I didn't want to start off with anything too personal for fear of scaring him away so I decided to ask about Laura first.

"Do you know Dave's girlfriend, Laura?" I said.

He snorted. "Yeah, I know Laura. Why?"

"She wasn't at the funeral."

Jake gave me a sudden look but didn't say anything.

"Do you know where she's from?" I said.

"Boston," Jake said in a sort of mock-elitist voice. I had to force myself not to smile.

"Do you have any idea why she wouldn't have gone to the funeral?"

He shrugged. "Maybe she doesn't know he's dead. She went home Thursday night. Dave drove her to the airport. Or," he added with a smirk, "maybe she does know and Daddy wouldn't let her come."

I frowned. "You mean Laura's father didn't like Dave?"

"Let's just say Senator Big Shot VanderHayden thought his precious daughter could do better. Bunch of lousy snobs."

"Hmm," I said, pursing my lips. "Do you know where I could reach her?"

Jake got up, pulled an address book from beneath a pile of

mail on top of the stereo, and handed it to me. I found the address and phone number and copied it onto the back of a credit card receipt I had in my pocket.

"How long was Dave going out with her?" I said.

"Couple of years, at least."

"Was her father aware that he was still seeing her?"

Jake looked at me without answering, but his face said, "How should I know?"

"You don't know?" I said.

He rolled his eyes. "No, I don't know. Okay?"

"What made you come back?" I asked carefully.

Jake looked at me, turned away, and shrugged. "It was Christmas," he said. "I didn't want my mom to be alone."

I smiled. "That was nice of you; she was really worried."

No response.

"Why weren't you at the funeral? Where were you?" I said.

Jake glared at me. "I was in Green Bay, playing blackjack, okay? It's not a crime, you know."

"So you didn't know about Dave until you got home?"

Jake stared out the window for a few moments, got up from the couch, and put an empty box on the coffee table. He started packing again, but this time in a very careful, measured manner.

"Did you know about Dave's death before you left?" I said again.

"I already explained all this to the cops," he said slowly. "Why don't you just leave it to them and stay out of it? You could end up like Dave."

I watched him intently for a few moments, trying to gauge his meaning, but he didn't vary his movements or his expression.

"Why do you say that?" I asked.

Jake stopped what he was doing and looked up at me. He closed his eyes and let out a deep breath.

"Look," he said as he opened them again. "I found him, okay? I found his body long before Janice did and I just freaked and took off." Jake's voice had a slight quaver. He looked away quickly and busied himself with his packing again.

I wrinkled my brow. "When did you find him?" I said.

"Friday night, around one o'clock, when I came back from the bars."

"Did you see anything that looked out of the ordinary?"

Jake looked at me like I had my head screwed on backward.

"I mean other than Dave," I said. "Did it look like someone had broken in, like they'd been searching for something? Anything like that?"

He frowned and thought for a while. "I don't think so," he said. "I didn't notice anything looking unusual."

"Nothing was wrong with the door lock or anything?"

"No, it was fine," Jake said. "I let myself in with my key and it worked just like it always does."

"No papers or anything strewn around the apartment? No drawers emptied on the beds? Nothing like that?"

Jake shook his head. "No, nothing. I would've noticed it."

"Why did you run when you saw the body, instead of calling the police?"

No answer, just an uncomprehending stare.

"I mean, didn't you think it was a suicide when you saw his body?"

"No, I didn't think it was a suicide," Jake said. "There's no way he would've killed himself. I was pretty sure I knew who did it, too, and I wasn't going to hang around so they could get me, too."

"You think you know who did it?" I said, my eyes opening wide. "Who? Who do you think did it?"

"I already told this to the police," Jake said.

"Well, tell me, too," I said. "Please, Jake."

Jake gave me a jaded look. "You really shouldn't be messin' around with these guys," he said. "You're just going to get yourself hurt."

I clenched my teeth and tried to remain calm. "Jake," I said. "Please. Just tell me. I'm not going to do anything stupid. Trust me."

Jake gave me one of those Oh-gosh-I-guess-I'll-have-to-humor-you looks. He was really starting to get on my nerves.

"It had to be the guys he borrowed money from," he said. "Those guys don't mess around when you don't pay them back."

I stared at him with my mouth open. "You're not saying he borrowed money from loan sharks, are you?" There was no way I was going to believe that one.

"All I know is, Dave told me he borrowed two thousand bucks off some guys and he was supposed to pay them back in a week. They must've been loan sharks. Who else lends money like that?"

"Jake," I said, growing exasperated, "it could've been anybody. Who's going to kill somebody for a measly two thousand bucks? Do you even know for sure Dave didn't pay them back?"

"Yeah, I know he didn't pay them back. He told me he didn't. He thought he was going to double it in a week but instead he lost it."

"How'd he lose it?" I said.

"Playing blackjack."

"Dave was a gambler, too?"

Jake rolled his eyes. "Dave was a blackjack *expert*, man. He had a method worked out that was practically foolproof."

"Well, if it was so foolproof," I said, "why'd he lose all the money?"

Jake sneered at me. "It just had a few bugs in it, that's all. He was still perfecting it."

I put my head in my hands.

"So maybe it wasn't the loan sharks," Jake said. "Maybe it was the guys from the casinos. They don't take too kindly to people who win a lot of money, you know, and they're all run by the mob." Jake adopted a tough-guy stance and gave me a look like he'd been around, and I hadn't.

I screwed up my face. "Jake, they're run by American Indians," I said. "Didn't you ever notice that?"

Jake stared off into space. "Oh, yeah," he said after a few moments.

"Do you have any Advil?" I said.

"No, why?"

"Never mind," I said. "Forget it. Did Dave ever talk to you about those bomb scares?"

"No," Jake said. "I don't know anything about that."

"What about his other friends? Do you know any of them?"

Jake shrugged. "I met a few of them. There's some guys he wrestled with—Scott Chapman, I think, and Dick Burghoff."

I wrote the names on the same credit card receipt I'd written Laura's name and number on.

I gazed out the window at the brick wall, trying to think of something else to ask him, but nothing came to mind.

"Jake, would you mind if I hang around for a while and look through Dave's things? I want a chance to check everything out before you move. When are you leaving?"

"End of January," Jake said, "if I can find another place. You can stay and look around if you want to, but I'm taking off, so lock the door when you're done."

"Okay," I said. "Thanks."

Chapter Six

Jake showed me to Dave's room and left a few minutes later, for which I was thankful. It'd be a lot easier to snoop without him peering over my shoulder.

The first thing that struck me about the room was the mess. Jake said nothing seemed out of place. If that were true, Dave was an absolute slob. The bed was unmade, and clothes were strewn everywhere. A dresser drawer was on the floor, the contents dumped out and scattered. The closet door was open. Clothes were pulled from hangers and left in a heap on the floor. A box, formerly full of odds and ends—notebooks, an old calculator, paperbacks—was overturned and emptied on top of the clothes.

The room was small and square, painted a dirty bluish-gray, with one small window. The nightstand next to the bed was oak, the varnish peeling away, and it was piled high with paperbacks and magazines. I looked through them but found nothing of interest. Most of the magazines were computer-oriented; the paperbacks were science fiction. There weren't any drawers.

An armchair was on the other side of the bed, covered with an old chenille bedspread. A pile of books and papers was on the seat and I sorted through them, too. Nothing. Just textbooks and school assignments.

The three-tier bookcase lining the window wall was one of those homemade things constructed of unfinished plywood and bricks. The top shelf held half a dozen wrestling trophies, the bottom two, a variety of textbooks, dictionaries, and other reference texts. There were also three large stacks of Dick Tracy comic books, a volume of Shakespeare's plays, books

71

on astronomy, computer languages, computer games, computer viruses, and computer hacks, and several on blackjack, sheepshead, and chess. Good grief.

What looked like an old school desk was pushed against another wall, with a computer and a bunch of papers on top. The drawers were open, the contents still inside, but somewhat messed up. The top side drawer contained several boxes of computer disks, the other two, computer printouts. The center drawer was locked.

Behind the desk, on the wall, was a bulletin board. Pushpins held snapshots, news clippings, various handwritten notes, and some postcards. Two of the snapshots were of a young woman, probably in her early twenties, with long, unstyled, medium-brown hair parted in the middle and pushed behind her ears. In both pictures, she wore jeans with holes in the knees and an oversized T-shirt. There was a relatively recent picture of Janice and Marge, sitting on Marge's front porch. They had their arms around each other and happy smiles on their faces. Another showed a much younger Marge with a tall, good-looking man, a young girl, and a small baby.

There were three news clippings. One had something to do with the validity of SAT scores reported by colleges and universities, another was about Medicaid fraud, and the third about a proposed shopping center to which East Side residents were objecting. The handwritten notes were just reminders of test dates and wrestling practices.

There were two postcards. One was a picture of the Eiffel Tower and the other a French bakery with small tables and chairs outside, next to the sidewalk. I removed both from the bulletin board so I could read what was written on the back. The card with the Eiffel Tower was undated and I couldn't make out the postmark. It read:

Dear Dave,

  I'm having a great time but I sure wish you were here with me. Maybe someday we can do this together. Dad's being a jerk, as usual. Can't wait to see you.

                                        Love,
                                        Laura

The other had a postmark from last April, and read:

Dear Dave,
I ate breakfast here this morning. Hope you like me chubby. I miss you. I really love you and can't wait to see you on Tuesday.

Love,
Laura

Interesting stuff, but nothing in the way of a clue as far as I could see. I put the cards back where I'd found them, sat on the bed, and looked around the room.

Where was the typewriter?

I was sure Janice had said the suicide note was in the typewriter. There was no typewriter in Dave's room and I didn't remember seeing one in the living room. I went back to the living room, looked everywhere there, and in the dining room. No typewriter.

I passed by Jake's room on the way back to Dave's, turned around, and went back. The door was closed. Hmm. I was pretty sure Jake wasn't coming back. What harm could it do to take just a teensy little peek? I opened the door—and gasped. There was an outline of a body on the rug and a typewriter on the desk. Well, I guess I know a clue when I see one.

I went back to Dave's room, sat down at the desk, and started to sort through the papers on top. There was nothing there but school assignments, old tests, and class notes. Well, that was about it for Dave's room. I went back to Jake's.

This time I went in and closed the door behind me. Jake's room was larger than Dave's and a little more cheery. Instead of dreary gray-blue, it was painted a clean, bright yellow. And there were colorful posters all over the walls. The carpeting was bright blue.

His bed was unmade, too, and covered with folded clothes, belts, and socks. There was a highboy chest with five drawers. I opened them one by one. Three were empty. The other two contained sweaters and underwear.

An old orange crate was next to the bed, with a lamp and a few books on top. Five more orange crates were under the window, turned on their sides and used as bookcases. The only other thing in the room was the desk. This one was gray metal with two side drawers and another in the middle. The side drawers held tests, school assignments, and class notes; the middle one, pens, paper clips, and the like. There was nothing on top of the desk but the typewriter and a page-a-day calendar. I flipped through the calendar. No entries.

The typewriter was an electric, fairly new, with no paper. I checked the ribbon to see if it was the type that retains an impression of everything that was typed, but it wasn't. I saw that on *Columbo* once—that's how he caught the killer. Oh, well.

I went back to Dave's room and sat down at the desk again. I suddenly remembered the center drawer. (I'll tell you, the next time one of my friends asks me to help her find a murderer, I'm going to be a lot more organized about it.)

I needed to find the key. I hadn't noticed one in any of the drawers, but there was a wooden jewelry box on top of the dresser. I got up and opened it. It appeared to be filled with nothing but change but underneath I found a key.

I went back to the desk. Darn. Wrong key. Out of sheer frustration, I gave the drawer a couple of hard shakes—and it opened!

The drawer was lined with brown paper and was empty except for a high school diploma. I took the diploma out and looked at it, checking to see if there was anything hidden inside. Nope. I put it back, but when I did, the brown paper moved and so did the piece of plywood to which it was attached. On the left upper edge, I could see what looked like a catalog or magazine poking out from underneath. I opened the drawer as far as I could, lifted the plywood, and removed it. It wasn't a catalog. It was a calendar. Inside the calendar was a bankbook. Underneath it were a computer printout and a letter.

The letter was from Laura. I started to open it and then put it back. It was probably just a personal love letter. I shouldn't be reading that kind of thing, should I? Oh, what the heck. I took it back out of the drawer. I had the letter out of the envelope when my conscience got the better of me again, and I put it back. It'd still be there, if I ever decided it might be important.

I opened the calendar instead, and paged through it. There were no entries at all for January. In February, he'd had a dentist appointment and gotten his hair cut. Good for him. On March seventeenth, he'd penned in *Party! Party! Party!* Nothing in April. May was blank, except for May twelfth—*Last day of classes!!* In June, he'd had an appointment with Dr. King. Then nothing for July all the way through October. In November, he'd circled Thanksgiving Day. In December, he'd circled the first and third Saturdays, and written *8:00* on the first Friday and *9:00* on the third. He had another appointment with Dr. King for the twenty-third. That was it. It didn't mean a darn thing to me, but I copied the entries on a blank sheet of paper and put the calendar back with the letter.

The bankbook was next. Now this was a little more interesting. His balance was relatively stable through September, and then, on October ninth, he made a withdrawal of five hundred dollars. He deposited twelve hundred on October twelfth. On October sixteenth he withdrew fifteen hundred, then deposited two thousand on the nineteenth. November sixth, he withdrew two thousand; November thirteenth, another five hundred. November twentieth he withdrew three hundred and November twenty-third, he deposited eight-fifty. There was nothing then until December fifth. On that date, he made a deposit of ten thousand dollars. On December eleventh, he withdrew eight thousand. That was the last transaction. I copied everything and put the book where I'd found it.

Now for the computer printout. Fat chance I was going to understand that. I opened it and let it trail to the floor. The thing was enormous, pages and pages of names, numbers, and dates. There were three columns. After every name was a number, meaning I didn't know what, and a date. There were no column headings so I couldn't tell what the numbers meant, although most of them were the same. The oddest thing was that every name, with its accompanying number and date, was recorded twice, one right after the other. It made no sense to me but I decided to take it with me since there was no way I could copy all the information.

I replaced the plywood and the diploma, made sure nothing was sticking out, and closed the drawer.

I looked at my watch. It was almost one-thirty. Mike ought to be up by now, even on a Saturday. I went to the living room and dialed his number. No answer. I tried my parents' house.

"Yes, he's here," my mom said. "Why? Is anything wrong?"

"No, Mom. I just want to ask him a computer question."

"Are you sure?" she said.

"Yes, Mom," I answered patiently. "I'm sure."

When Mike came to the phone I told him not to let on where I was and what I was doing and then I gave him a quick explanation.

"Now. Can you tell me how to work a computer over the phone?" I said.

"Well, it depends on what you mean," he said. "What do you want to do?"

"Well, first, how do you turn it on?"

I heard him grunt in disgust. "You're kidding, right?"

"No, Mike, I'm not kidding. You know I don't know anything about computers. That's why I'm calling you."

He sighed loudly. "It has an on/off switch," he said in his most condescending voice. "Just find it and turn it on. Look in the back, if you don't see one in front."

"Okay," I said, trying not to let my anger show. "Hold on."

I ran into Dave's room, found the switch, and turned it on. It made a familiar computer-type noise, so I grabbed one of the computer disks and went back to the phone.

"Okay, I'm back. Now, listen. He has a whole bunch of these little computer disks. Can you tell me how to put them in the computer and look at them?"

"Get a pencil and paper," Mike said with a groan. After he told me what to do, I hung up and got to work.

The first disk (excuse me, diskette) had some sort of school project on it. The one after that looked like a compilation of all his grades, from every course, through all four years of college. Every last one was an A. Now why would he need a record of that? Maybe he just liked looking at all those As.

The next two were course outlines. The one after that was a record of his medical bills, and the next, a record of his monthly expenses. I put those two aside. There were three more course outlines, several school projects and papers, and about ten I didn't understand at all.

I called Mike back.

"How do I print something out?" I said.

He sighed loudly, again, and gave me step-by-step instructions in a voice you might use to explain sharing to a two-year-old. What a jerk.

I printed out the medical bills and the monthly expenses, put everything back where I'd found it (with the exception of the printout I was "borrowing"), and left for home. It was time to call Laura VanderHayden.

When I got home it was almost three. I called Janice right away, and then Laura. A woman, whom I judged to be a housekeeper, picked up on the third ring.

"VanderHayden residence," she said. She was using an extremely formal voice, sort of butler-like, and it had an annoying nasal quality.

"Miss VanderHayden is not home at present," she said when I asked for Laura. I left a message asking Laura to call me as soon as she could, and said only that it concerned Dave Grezinski. When she asked me to spell "Grezinski" she pronounced it like it was a dirty word she'd never heard before.

I went to the refrigerator and opened it. No juice, no fruit, no vegetables, no eggs, no milk. No nothing. I had to go to the store. I exhaled loudly, put on my coat, and got in the car. I was a little reluctant to leave the house again, in case Laura should call, but Sendik's is only a few blocks away, on Oakland. If I really worked at it, I could make it back in no time at all.

For a grocery store, Sendik's is pretty neat. I actually went to law school with a guy who met his wife there. They have all kinds of little gourmet things and their produce section is wonderful. I picked up a loaf of French bread, some fresh onion rolls, cheddar and pepper jack cheeses, the makings for a salad, some mangoes, kiwis, apples, and bananas. I added some skim milk, two kinds of juice, a carton of eggs, threw in a package of store-made beef-and-onion pastry things that looked really good, and I was done. I got through the checkout line, put the groceries in the car, and was back home within half an hour of the time I'd left.

As soon as I got in the door, I checked my messages. There was one, but it was from a client. I put the groceries away, returned the call to my client, and then made myself a cup of tea and a sandwich of pepper jack cheese on an onion roll with lots of mustard. I gathered all my "evidence" together and sat at the kitchen table sorting through it as I ate. I made a list of things I'd found out and questions I had, using a sort of stream-of-consciousness method, just writing down whatever came to mind. I read it over twice after I'd finished, but it didn't trigger any great flashes of brilliance, so I put it away.

I was restless. It was Saturday, I didn't feel like working, but I wanted to get something accomplished. If only I had a suspect, I could stake out his house. Or follow him in my car. Well, I didn't have one, so I decided to do some laundry instead. I left my list et al. on the kitchen table, went upstairs, collected a basketful of dirty clothes, and brought it down to the basement. I have two rooms down there. The one farthest from the steps has a washer and dryer, furnace, fuse boxes, and all that sort of thing. The one right at the bottom of the stairs is carpeted and furnished, with a couch, three big easy chairs, a TV, and a pool table. There's a play area for the kids with a big box of toys my Aunt Sarah had kept for us to play with when we were small. And there's a nice little powder room and a shower. I put the laundry in, started the cycle, and went back up.

On my way back to the second floor for another load, I took my "Dave" file to the library to put in my desk. My message light was on—it was Laura VanderHayden! She must have called when I was downstairs. I couldn't believe it. I called her right back. A maid-type answered again, but this time it was a different voice. Ms. VanderHayden has stepped out, I was told, and might she take a message? I asked her to please tell Ms. VanderHayden that Ms. Hartley was returning her call. So much for that.

I went upstairs, put as much laundry as I could fit into the basket, went back down to the basement, and sorted, while I tried to imagine what Laura VanderHayden's life was like. I had visions of maids and butlers and other assorted domestics bustling about, cleaning and shining, dusting and waxing, doing all the laundry and putting everything away. Dinners were served at a mile-long table with candles and silver and crystal and everyone in formal dress. When Miss VanderHayden "stepped out" she was transported in a gleaming Rolls Royce by a uniformed chauffeur, who took her wherever she wanted to go and waited for her in the car until she was through.

The chauffeur.

James? Or Charles, maybe. Tall, dark, and handsome. Young. Virile. Forbidden. Now, who can resist forbidden? Laura has an affair with Chuck the chauffeur, gets bored, breaks it off, goes back to Dave, and Chuck kills him in a fit of envy. Well, things like that do happen, you know.

After the laundry, I did some knitting and reading, had the beef-and-onion pastries for supper (they were good), read some more, and went to bed. Laura didn't return my call that night.

The next day was Sunday, December twenty-seventh—the day I met Mrs. Robinson. I called Janice just to see how she was doing. I told her I wanted to show her the computer printout to see if it meant anything to her. She said she'd be in to work the next morning and she'd do it then.

I called Emily next, but she wasn't home. I was caught up enough with my work that I didn't need to do anything, and I was still feeling restless. I went to the library and got out the "Dave" file, and looked through everything I had. Still no ideas. I made a list of the people I hadn't talked to: Dr. King, Dave's wrestling coach, Scott Chapman, Dick Burghoff, Laura, Laura's father, Dave's employer.

Who else might know something? I had a sudden thought. I could question the people in Dave's apartment building. One of the doors was ajar when I went to see Jake, the one right next door, wide open. Maybe someone had seen or heard something that night, or some other time.

I called Jake to tell him what I was doing and he said he'd buzz me in when I got there. I grabbed a notebook and a pen and I was gone.

The sky was completely overcast, not a hint of sun. I hadn't called the weather but I could tell the temperature was well below zero. The snow near the sides of the streets was black now, which added a lot to the overall effect of the day. Darn depressing.

Jake let me in and I went straight to the third floor, figuring the people there were the only ones likely to have witnessed anything. I knocked on Jake's door first, and told him I had some more questions for him but I'd have to do it some other time since I'd forgotten to bring along the computer printout.

"Call anytime," he said.

The door to the apartment next door was wide open again and I could hear someone moving about inside, probably in the kitchen from the sound of things. I knocked several times, and pretty loudly, but there was no response.

"Hello," I called out, and knocked again.

The kitchen noises stopped and I could hear someone walking—shuffling, actually—toward the doorway. It took close to a minute before she came into view. She was elderly, as I had guessed, probably in her eighties, maybe even nineties. She was tall, but hunched over so badly she had to raise her head to look at me. Snow-white hair, very sparse, soft and wavy. Brown eyes, but a lighter shade of brown than I think I've ever seen.

Her hands were knotted and twisted, covered with veins and brown spots. Her face was like a crumpled piece of paper, but probably as soft as silk, I thought.

"Hang on," she said with a smile and a wobbly voice. "I'm not as spry as I was in my youth."

She made walking a few yards look like running a marathon, but she was so good-natured about it I couldn't help smiling.

When she reached me, she raised her head and squinted. "Do I know you, dear?" she said.

I smiled. "No, you don't," I said. "I'm sorry to cause you so much trouble. I was hoping I could ask you a few questions about something that happened in the apartment next door the Friday before Christmas."

"Oh, dear me, yes. That poor boy."

She was starting to totter so I suggested we sit down. She gave me a grateful smile.

"That might be a good idea," she said. "I've been on my feet for quite some time and I could do with a rest. Would you mind helping me to my chair?"

"Sure," I said, and guided her by the elbow to a chair near the couch. It was a plush armchair, upholstered in a faded green fabric with tiny pink roses in the foreground, a crocheted doily hanging over the back. When she was seated and comfortable, I sat on the couch directly across from her.

"Are you the boy's family?" she asked.

"No, but I'm a very close friend of his sister."

"May I offer you some tea, dear?" she said.

"Oh, no, thank you," I said. "If you'd like something, I'd be happy to get it for you, though." I hated to think of her walking all the way back to the kitchen.

"No, thank you," she said. "I've already had mine. But you're very kind to offer."

"My name is Beth Hartley, by the way. I'm sorry, I forgot to introduce myself."

"Don't apologize, my dear. When you get to be my age, some days you'll forget your own name. But today I remember. I'm May Robinson," she said with a warm smile.

"I'm glad to meet you," I said.

She looked at me curiously then. "Are you married?"

I laughed. "No, I'm not. I was, but my second husband died ten years ago."

"Oh, dear. I'm very sorry. Do you work?"

I told her about my business and she seemed utterly fascinated. "My stars," she said. "My stars. Well, good for you. I like to see you young women making your own way in the world. Not many of us did that in my day. If I had to do it all over again I think I'd do things differently."

I smiled. "What would you do?" I said.

She looked at me with a twinkle in her eye. "I'd be a doctor," she said. "I'd go to college and become a doctor."

"That's what I'm planning to do in my next life," I said with a laugh.

"Maybe I'll wait for you," she said. "We'll do it together."

"It's a date," I said, grinning.

"Now, my dear. Let's get down to business. What did you want to ask me?"

"Well, I noticed that your door was open the other day when I was here, and today, too. Did you have it open last Friday night, by any chance?"

"I generally keep it open until I retire at ten," Mrs. Robinson said. "I can't recall specifically, but I imagine I kept it open until ten that night as I usually do."

"Do you remember hearing or seeing anything unusual?"

She considered that for a few moments. "On that Friday. No. I can't say that I do. Of course, I don't remember well, as I told you."

"Do you remember seeing anyone come or go? Anyone walk by your door?"

She frowned. "I remember seeing a delivery boy with a pizza box walk by a while back. But I can't be sure what day that was."

"Did you ever hear any arguing next door?" I said.

"Well, yes, I did. Although I couldn't make out what was being said. I don't hear so well, either. Warranty's run out on all my parts," she said with a chuckle.

I laughed. "Do you remember when it was that you heard the argument?"

Mrs. Robinson slowly shook her head, something which seemed to take some effort on her part. "Could've been anytime," she said. "I'm sorry I can't remember better. I'm afraid I'm not much help to you."

"You're a big help," I said.

She gave me an appreciative grin, then wrinkled her brow. "My neighbor friend told me the boy committed suicide," she said. "What is it you're trying to find out, if you don't mind my prying?"

"Oh, no, of course not," I said. "I'm trying to find out if it was actually a murder. His sister, Janice, is sure it was and I really think so, too, at this point."

"Oh, my stars," she said. "Oh, my stars. Well, now I understand. Oh, my."

"You know, I'm a little concerned about your keeping your door open," I said, "especially if it was open when the murderer was here. It might be a lot safer for you if you kept it closed."

Worry lines formed on her face. "Oh, dear," she said. "Maybe you're right. I do like having it open, though. It makes me feel less lonely."

"Do you have any family?" I asked.

"I have a daughter, Marie, but she lives in Florida now. She comes to visit a few times a year, but that leaves a lot of time in between." Mrs. Robinson looked up at me. "I wish you'd come to visit me again," she said. "I enjoy your company."

"I'd love to," I said, fighting against the lump I felt in my throat. "If you'd like, I'll come to see you every week until you get sick and tired of me and throw me out."

"Oh, my dear girl," she said. "You're an angel if there

ever was one. I'll so look forward to that every week. We'll choose a special day, any one you like.''

I grinned and thought for a moment. ''How about Sundays? Would you like that?''

''Splendid,'' she said. ''Splendid. Sundays. I can hardly wait. What day is this?''

''Sunday,'' I said, smiling. ''See, we've started already. I'll give you a card with my name and number and you call me if you need something in the meantime, okay? You have a phone, don't you?''

''Yes. Right on my dressing table next to the bed. I'll give you my phone number, too. We'll be just like two girlfriends, won't we?''

''Yes, we will,'' I said, and gave her a hug. ''I'll call you on Saturday and we'll decide on a time. In the meanwhile, will you promise me to keep your door closed, at least until this man is caught?''

''I'll lock up right after you leave,'' she said.

I helped her to the door. ''Who is the neighbor friend who told you it was a suicide?'' I said after I stepped outside.

''Mrs. Markham in 309. Just tell her May sent you,'' Mrs. Robinson said with a kind smile. ''I'll look so forward to seeing you, my dear.''

''I will, too,'' I said, and gave her another hug. When she closed her door, I had to wipe a few tears from my eyes.

I hadn't taken any notes while I talked to Mrs. Robinson, so I stood in the hall and wrote down everything she'd told me, so I wouldn't forget. Then I knocked on number 309. Mrs. Markham was younger, probably no more than sixty. She was tall, maybe five-five, about thirty pounds overweight. Her hair was a dark, coarse gray, worn short and close to her head. She wore bright green sweatpants, a matching sweatshirt, and hot pink feathery house slippers. She greeted me with a big smile.

''Well, now. What can I do for you?'' she said, giving me a look like I was a little girl.

I told her who I was, said that Mrs. Robinson had sent me, and explained what I wanted.

"Come on in," she said. "I'd be glad to talk to you. Just sit yourself down; I have something on the stove." She hurried out of the room at a sort of modified jogging pace, her slippers flapping against her feet as she went.

She came back in a minute, looking a little winded. She sat down in a blue vinyl recliner across from the couch on which I was sitting. The couch was upholstered in blue vinyl, too. The whole room was weird. The floor was bare, hardwood like Jake's, although the finish was in better shape. The throw rugs she'd scattered about were all different, some red, two green, one a bright orange. At least two of them were meant for a bathroom. The walls were the same off-white stucco as in the other apartments, but hers were decorated with mirrors—five in all, each a different size. She didn't have any plants. Thank goodness.

"How's May doing today?" she asked when she'd caught her breath.

"Fine," I said, smiling. "She's really very nice."

"Yes, she is," Mrs. Markham said. "She has no one in town so I try to look in on her whenever I can."

I told her I'd talked May into closing her door.

"I've been telling her that for years," she said. "You must've put some kind of spell on her to get her to do that."

"Well, I'm afraid I probably just frightened her," I said. "But I am worried she may have had her door open when whoever did this showed up. If he noticed it, he might think she knows something."

Mrs. Markham took a deep breath and let it out. "Oh, Lord," she said.

"He was killed on Friday, but they didn't discover the body until Saturday," I said. "Do you remember seeing or hearing anything unusual either Friday or Saturday?"

"I remember Saturday real well," she said. "There was an awful lot of commotion when they found him, police coming in and out and all. I believe I saw his sister and his mama. The young one was crying her eyes out, pretty near hysterical with grief. I believe his mama was just in shock. Didn't even know what to do with herself, poor thing. It's a horrible business.''

I sighed and nodded. ''Can you remember anything at all about Friday?''

She put a look on her face to show she was thinking hard. ''I think I saw one of the boys who live there,'' she said. ''Not the one who was killed. The other one.''

''Do you remember what time that was?''

She thought for a moment, and nodded her head. ''Yes. It was right before the program I always watch on Friday nights. A few minutes before eight.''

''Was he coming or going?'' I said.

''Coming. Walked right by me and didn't say a word, same as always.''

''May said she heard arguing coming from their apartment sometime or another. Did you ever hear anything like that?''

''I heard one of them screaming at someone,'' she said. ''On the telephone, I assumed, since I only heard the one voice. But that was way back, probably over a month ago.''

''Do you know which one it was?''

Mrs. Markham shook her head. ''No, I wouldn't know which one unless I'd seen him.''

''Could you hear what was said?''

She raised her eyebrows. ''He was telling someone to mind his own blankety-blank business and to stay out of his life.'' Mrs. Markham's face said, *I'm sure I don't have to fill in the blanks, do I?*

''Is that all you heard?'' I said.

''I was just walking by, coming back from the supermarket. I didn't hear anything else and frankly I didn't want to. Those boys ought to have their mouths washed out with soap.''

I laughed. ''Would you do me a favor?'' I said. ''I'll leave you my number and if you think of anything at all, would you call me?''

''I sure will,'' she said. ''I'm sorry I couldn't be more help.''

"That's quite all right," I said. "I really appreciate your talking to me."

I checked my watch when I was back in the hallway. It was almost noon. I was getting tired and hungry but it was Sunday and the most likely time to find people home, I figured. I made a few notes regarding my conversation with Mrs. Markham, and knocked on number 310, the door I'd seen ajar when I first visited Jake. There was no one at home. I made a note on my pad to come back another day.

Next, I tried the door on the other side of Jake's. A young guy answered, late twenties, with shoulder-length, dark blond hair, a scruffy beard, and bloodshot eyes. Six feet tall, maybe a hundred and thirty pounds, no muscle at all. He wore dirty jeans and a wrinkled T-shirt frayed around the neck.

"Can I help you?" he said, in a genuinely polite and friendly voice. It took me by surprise and I'm afraid it showed.

I grinned at him and he grinned back. I told him the whole story and he asked me to come in. His name was Gordon Kohn.

Gordon offered me a seat on his couch, which was worn, actually threadbare, but clean and neat like everything else in his apartment. He had the same layout as Jake, but he had more furniture and there was a more permanent look to the place, as if he intended to stay a while. The walls were covered with pictures, all prints framed inexpensively, but they were nice. A couple of Monets, a Utrillo (which I love), and some Renoirs (which I also love). He had bookshelves (real ones), a stereo, a TV, and a dining room table and chairs.

I told him how nice I thought it looked and admired his pictures. He flashed me a shy but very pleased grin. "Thanks," he said. "I like it, too. I hope you'll excuse my appearance. I just got home from work and I haven't had a chance to clean up."

"What do you do?" I said.

"I work at a garden center," he said. "I'm planning to open one of my own someday." He looked so proud, it made me smile.

"That's great," I said.

"Can I offer you something?" he said. "A Coke or some coffee?"

I smiled. "A Coke would be great. I'm dying of thirst."

"I'll be right back," he said. "Just make yourself at home."

He came back with two Cokes and two glasses, handed one of each to me, and sat down.

"Do you know Dave and Jake at all?" I asked.

Gordon shrugged. "Not really," he said. "I say hello when I see them but that's about it. I'm not home much anyway."

"Were you home the Friday night before Christmas? They found Dave on Saturday but he was killed sometime Friday night."

"I was home until around seven, but then I took my girl-friend to a movie and didn't get back until about one."

"Did you see or hear anything before you left or after you came home?"

Gordon shrugged. "Nothing unusual," he said. "I saw one of them coming home from somewhere. The one with the dark hair."

"That's Jake," I said. "Dave was blond. Did he say any-thing to you?"

"He said 'hi' like he always does."

"Did he look strange in any way?"

Gordon laughed. "He looked a little drunk, but other than that he seemed normal enough."

"Have you ever heard anything weird going on next door? Any arguing, or anything like that?"

He shook his head. "No, I really haven't," he said. "But like I said, I'm not home much. I work a lot of hours and then I try to spend as much time as I can with my girlfriend. Fi-ancée, I should say, as of Christmas." He grinned, and turned a light shade of pink.

"Congratulations," I said. "She's very lucky."

"Naw, I'm the lucky one," Gordon said.

I shook my head, still smiling. The building appeared to be filled with such warm, genuine people, but there'd been a murder in their midst. For some reason, that made it seem all the more gruesome.

Gordon asked me what I did, and we talked about that for a while. I gave him one of my cards as I was leaving, and asked him to call me if he thought of anything he hadn't told me. He said he would.

I tried three more apartments after that, the ones nearest to Jake's, but no one answered. I thought of stopping by Jake's then, but I was too hungry to put off eating any longer. I decided to call him from home instead. I really wanted to talk to him about the stuff I'd found in the apartment. It's a good thing I did, too. He picked right up on something I hadn't even noticed.

Chapter Seven

It was after four when I got home. I made myself a salad and an omelette with onions and sweet peppers and paged through my notes while I ate. I reread my stream-of-consciousness list and made from it a new list of things I needed to ask Jake. As soon as I'd finished eating, I called him.

"Yeah," he said.

"Jake, it's Beth," I said. "Are you busy? I just wanted to ask you a few questions."

I heard him sigh. "Shoot," he said.

"Did Dave gamble a lot?"

"Depends on what you mean by a lot," Jake said.

"Well, how often did he do it, let's put it that way?"

"For a while he was going every weekend. Depended on what else he had going, you know?"

"Do you have any idea how much money he made or lost?"

"Sometimes a lot, sometimes not so much."

I let out a deep breath. "Could you give me some idea how much you're talking about?" I said.

"I . . . oh, I don't know. It varied. Sometimes he'd win real big and sometimes he'd lose everything. Depends on the night."

"What's real big?" I said. "Can you give me some numbers?"

"Couple of thousand, I guess."

"Did he ever win as much as ten thousand dollars?"

Jake laughed. "No way," he said. "I would've heard about that one."

"How about losses?" I said. "Did he ever lose more than five thousand?"

"No," Jake said, starting to sound impatient. "I told you, the most he ever lost was a couple of thousand. Far as I know, anyway."

"Do you know if he ever borrowed as much as ten thousand dollars from anyone?"

"Not that I know of. What's the big deal about the ten thousand dollars?"

"Oh, he made a deposit in that amount to his savings account on December fifth," I said.

"Sorry, can't tell you nothin' about it," Jake said. "It's news to me."

"Okay, that's fine," I said. "You're doing great. Okay, I also found a calendar in his desk and he had the dates December fifth and December nineteenth circled, and then he wrote 'eight o'clock' on December fourth and 'nine o'clock' on December eighteenth. Both of those were Fridays. Does any of that mean anything to you?"

"Well, wasn't he killed on December eighteenth?"

I slapped myself on the forehead. "Oh, of course," I said. "That's right. How could I forget that?"

I suddenly thought of something I hadn't asked Jake before. "Did you see Dave at all that day?" I said.

"Yeah, I saw him in the morning before I took off."

"Did you see him before you went out that night?"

"No, he wasn't home then," Jake said.

"Do you remember what time you left?"

Jake hesitated a few moments. "It was probably around eight-thirty," he said. "I was meeting someone at nine so I would've had to leave around then."

"Okay, so he could've had someone at the apartment at nine and you wouldn't have seen him, right?"

"Yeah, that's right. You think it was the killer?" He sounded incredulous and excited at the same time.

"Could be," I said. "Did Dave know what time you were going out?"

Jake thought for a while. "Yeah. I think he asked me that morning what I was doing later."

"Okay," I said. "Two more questions. Do you have the phone numbers for Scott Chapman and Dick Burghoff?"

"Hold on, I'll look in the address book.

"Got 'em," he said when he returned to the phone. He gave me both numbers, and their addresses, too.

"Great," I said. "Thanks."

"Anything else I can do you for?"

I laughed. "Not right now, thanks. But I do want to show you that computer printout I told you about and see if it means anything to you. Maybe sometime this week?"

"Sounds good to me. Just let me know."

"Okay. Thanks, Jake."

"No problem," he said. I could've sworn he was beginning to like me.

It was almost five. I hadn't exercised in a couple of days so I NordicTracked for my usual twenty minutes plus another ten. Then I made myself a bowl of popcorn with butter and salt and watched videos for the rest of the night. I checked my messages before I went up. None. Laura VanderHayden hadn't returned my last call. Was she avoiding me, or what?

The next day was Monday, December twenty-eighth. Dave's cardiologist had asked me to call his office first thing that morning so I did just that. I got up at seven, showered and dressed, ate breakfast, and dialed his office at eight. Too early. His service said no one would be there before nine.

Both Emily and Janice showed up around eight-thirty, within five minutes of each other, and Mrs. Gunther at ten to nine. We sat in the kitchen and chatted for a while, and then everyone went to work. I told Janice and Emily I'd be in after I made a few phone calls.

I dialed Dr. King's office again, and this time a receptionist picked up. She was expecting me, just as he'd promised.

"The doctor will see you at five-thirty tomorrow evening, if that is convenient," she said crisply.

"That would be great," I said, and hung up with a smile.

I tried Scott Chapman next. There was something about his name that seemed familiar but I couldn't quite place it. It'd been bugging me ever since Jake had mentioned him.

"Hello," said a groggy voice.

"Is this Scott Chapman?" I said.

"Yeah, this is Scott," he said.

"I'm sorry if I woke you," I said. "I guess I forget everyone doesn't have to get up as early as I do."

I could hear him yawn. "Oh, that's okay. No problem. What time is it, anyway?"

"About nine-fifteen."

"Boy, you *do* get up early."

I laughed. "I'm sorry. My name is Beth Hartley. I understand you were a pretty good friend of Dave Grezinski."

"Oh, yeah," Scott said, sounding sad. "I was."

"I'm a friend of his sister and she believes he was murdered. She asked me to help her prove it. That's why I'm calling. I was hoping you might be able to help me."

"How?" Scott asked.

"Just talk to me, tell me what you knew about his life, what he was like, that sort of thing."

"Sure," he said. "I can do that. I had a lot of trouble believing he did it myself. I just can't see it. What did you have in mind?"

"I don't know. Could I buy you lunch?"

"Sure," he said.

"Are you free today?"

"I have to be somewhere at three, but I'm free before that."

"Do you like Mexican?" I said.

"Love it," Scott said. "Have you ever been to La Casita?"

"Yeah, like about a million times. Meet you there, say twelve-thirty?"

"I'll be there with bells on," he said. (I've never understood what that means.)

"Hey, how will I know who you are?" he said then.

"Oh, right. Well, I'm five feet tall, normal weight, light brown shoulder-length hair, sort of blue-green eyes—but they change color so just ignore that."

He laughed. "Okay. Well, if I get there first, just look for the exceedingly handsome guy with the awesome body and piercing black eyes."

"Gee, I can hardly wait," I said, laughing.

I called Laura VanderHayden next. Not home. Wonderful. I left a message with the maid.

I worked until twelve-ten, ran upstairs, threw on my olive green corduroy slacks and one of the sweaters I made (it's a light plum Icelandic type with an olive green and ivory design), pulled my hair back with a burgundy bow-clip, and left for La Casita. That day, the sky was a deep blue, sun glistening everywhere. The kind of day that makes you feel glad to be you. The restaurant's on Farwell, very close to where I live. The food is fantastic, the atmosphere uplifting. I love the sound of Mexican music and the ethnic decor. I try to imagine I'm in Cancún or Puerto Vallarta whenever I'm there.

I arrived about ten minutes early but had to park a few blocks down, on a side street, which required several trips around the block until I found a space (all the streets are one-way). Scott hadn't arrived yet, according to the woman who showed me to my table. I ordered a strawberry seltzer and waited, enjoying the escape.

Several minutes later, a young man about six feet tall, maybe a little less, with wavy black hair, dark eyes, and gleaming white teeth, walked in, spoke to the hostess, and was directed to my table. He flashed me a truly disarming grin and held out his hand.

"I'm Scott Chapman," he said.

"Hi, I'm Beth." That's all I said. I was tongue-tied. He really was exceedingly handsome. He really did have an awesome body. And his eyes—wow. Too bad he was at least twenty years too young for me.

"Sorry I'm late," he said. "I got a phone call right when I was about to leave."

"That's okay," I said. The waitress came to the table just then, took Scott's drink order, and left.

"So how did you know Dave?" he asked, eyeing me with undisguised curiosity.

"I'm a good friend of his sister," I said. "She was my secretary when I worked for a law firm and I took her with me when I started my own business. I never actually met Dave."

He asked me about my business then, so we talked about that until the waitress returned with his drink and took our lunch order.

"How did you meet Dave?" I asked Scott when the waitress left.

"We were on the wrestling team together at Marquette," he said.

"Were you in any classes with him?"

"No," Scott said. "I'm premed and he was a computer sciences major. We didn't have any classes in common."

"Did you ever meet his roommate, Jake Grossman?"

"I met him once when I was over at Dave's place."

"How about any of his other friends?"

Scott shrugged. "Not really," he said. "Except for Dick Burghoff. He's the only other guy from the wrestling team he really hung around with."

I nodded.

"So you really think he was murdered?" Scott asked.

"Well, it sure looks that way. There are a lot of things that wouldn't make sense if it was a suicide, and Janice and Jake both say he'd never kill himself. How do you feel about that?"

"The same way," Scott said. "It just doesn't fit. He had plans. I'm talking big plans. A business, getting married, the whole bit. He just had too much going for him. The guy was brilliant at what he did. Just ask my dad. Dave was working for him for less than a week and already my dad was saying he was some kind of a genius."

The light bulb went on, and I slapped my forehead with the heel of my hand. "That's why your name sounded so familiar to me," I said. "You're the son of the doctor Dave worked for."

"Yes, that's right," Scott said. "I guess I just assumed you knew that. I was the one who introduced them. Dad had been talking for almost a year about hiring someone to put all of his records on computer so I told him about Dave because that was the kind of business he was planning to start. He did a great job for my dad. He just raved about him."

"I know this is kind of a personal question," I said, "but do you happen to know how much your dad paid him?"

Scott's eyebrows went up almost imperceptibly and he remained silent.

"Actually, what I'm really interested in knowing is whether it could have been as much as ten thousand dollars. I have a good reason for asking."

Scott looked incredulous. "It couldn't have been that much," he said. "He only worked for him a couple of months, part-time, and he wasn't even finished with the job."

"Did Dave ever talk to you about his gambling?" I asked.

Scott wrinkled his brow. "Gambling?" he said. "What kind of gambling?"

"Blackjack?"

He shook his head, the frown still on his face.

"Did he ever mention anything about the bomb scares?"

Scott exhaled sharply. "No, he never mentioned it," he said. "That whole thing was really bizarre. I can't believe he'd pull something like that."

"Did he ever say anything to you about owing money?"

Scott shrugged, and shook his head. "No, not really," he said. "I mean, he said he was glad for the work from my dad because he could always use the extra cash but it was nothing like he was in desperate need for it."

I nodded. The waitress returned with our food and we busied ourselves with that for a few minutes.

"Did he ever give you the impression that something was going on with him? Something that worried him or bothered him in any way?" I said a little later.

"Not that I noticed," Scott said. "I didn't really see him

that much, though. Not lately, anyway. He was using a lot of his free time to work for my dad.''

"So, you're premed, huh?''

Scott nodded and attempted a humble smile.

"Are you planning to practice with your dad when you get out of medical school?''

"I hope so,'' he said. "He could really use the help. He must work eighty, ninety hours a week since his partner died last year.''

"What kind of practice does he have?''

"Family, general practice.''

I smiled. "Well, that's great,'' I said. "I wish you luck.''

"Thanks,'' he said.

"Didn't you say Dave was planning to get married?''

"Yeah, he had some girl he'd been seeing for a couple of years. I met her once. She was pretty cool.''

"Was her name Laura?''

"Yeah, Laura Vanheusen or something like that.''

"VanderHayden,'' I said.

"Yeah, that's it. They were going to get married right after graduation.''

"Did Dave ever say anything to you about her dad objecting to them getting married?''

Scott laughed. "Yeah, the guy was a real jerk, I guess. I think they were going to just elope and tell everyone after the fact so it'd be too late to stop them.''

"You never met her father, did you?''

He frowned. "No, I think he lives in Boston.''

"Yeah, he does. I just thought he might've come to visit Laura.''

"Well, not that I know of,'' Scott said with a shrug.

"Can you think of anything else that might help?'' I said. "Anything I haven't thought of?''

"Not right off,'' he said. "If I do, I'll let you know, thought.''

I smiled. "Okay, that'd be great,'' I said. I took one of my cards from my wallet and handed it to him.

We'd finished eating and it was a little past one-thirty. "Would you like coffee or anything?" I asked.

"No, thanks," Scott said. "I'd better get going, anyway."

"Well, I really appreciate your coming and talking to me. You've been a big help."

"Happy to be of service," he said with a charming grin.

Scott waited for me while I paid the bill, and we walked out together.

"You should talk to my dad," he said. "He might be able to tell you something."

"I was planning to," I said. "Maybe I'll call him when I get home." Little did I know then how much I was going to enjoy *that* conversation.

"Tell him I said 'hi,' " Scott said with a smile.

"Okay, I will."

We were parked in different directions so I said good-bye, thanked him again, and took my time walking to my car. The day was beautiful, unusual for winter, and it was actually pleasant being outside.

When I got to the car, I decided to stop at The WoolWorks before I went home. That's my favorite yarn store, also on Farwell. I parked on Kane, walked a block down, and spent a leisurely thirty minutes looking through knitting patterns and choosing some yarn.

I drove home along Lincoln Memorial Drive, enjoying the lake view. The water close to shore was frozen, waves caught in mid-air, but the sun sparkled off the surface and made me think of spring.

When I got home, Janice was in the kitchen, eating her lunch.

"Hey, did you ever meet Scott Chapman?" I asked.

"I don't think so," she said, frowning. "Who's he?"

"One of Dave's wrestling buddies. I just had lunch with him. He's the son of the Dr. Chapman Dave was working for."

"Oh, yeah, that's right. That's how Dave got the job. What did he say?"

"Well . . . he said Dave and Laura were planning to get married right after graduation."

Janice gaped at me. "He never even told me that. He never even let me meet her." She turned away from me with a wounded look.

"I'm sorry," I said. "I think the only reason they were keeping it a secret was because of her father. He wasn't too keen on the idea."

Janice's response was a cross between a sneer and a wince.

"Scott also said his dad absolutely raved about Dave's work. Said he was some kind of a genius."

Now I got a happy smile, a proud big-sister look flashing across her face.

"He's a nice kid, too. I can see why Dave liked him."

She smiled again, gratitude erasing most of her anger.

"I think I'm going to call his dad today," I said. "I want to see if I can arrange to see him, although it looks like he's so busy he may never have time."

Janice nodded. "Dave said he had a lot of patients."

"Oh, I just remembered something," I said. "I wanted to show you that stuff I found in Dave's apartment."

I went to the library, retrieved my file, and showed Janice everything I had. None of it meant anything to her, although she wondered where Dave had gotten all that money.

When Janice went back to the library, I put in a call to Dr. Chapman's office. I left my name and number with his receptionist and asked that he call me regarding Dave Grezinski if he had the chance.

I worked until Janice and Emily left at five o'clock, then brought my brief into the kitchen and worked some more. My phone rang at seven-thirty.

It was Dr. Chapman. I couldn't believe it.

"I'm sorry I took so long to get back to you," he said. "I've been pretty backed up here."

"Oh, don't apologize," I said. "I know how busy you must be. I'm grateful to you for taking the time to call me at all."

He laughed. "That's quite all right," he said. "Now what can I do for you?"

He had a soft, easy voice, the sort that makes you feel you've known someone forever. If he looks anything like his son, I thought, I'm going to be in big trouble.

"I was hoping to talk to you about Dave Grezinski," I said. "If you can spare any time at all, I promise I'll try to keep it short."

"I'll make the time," he said. "I understand from my son, Scott, that you suspect he's been murdered?"

"Yes, that's right. His sister Janice asked me to help her prove it, so I'm looking for any information that might help."

"Have you had dinner yet?" he said.

"Uh . . . no, I haven't. I've been working."

He laughed, a soft, easy laugh, just like his voice. "Then we're two of a kind," he said. "I'll tell you what. I just saw my last patient for the day and I was about to get a bite to eat. How about if I take you to dinner and we can talk then? I usually eat alone, and I'd love the company."

"Sure, that'd be nice," I said. "Shall I meet you somewhere?"

"Let's make it Karl Ratzsch's. I feel like splurging."

"Hey, that'd be great."

"Would eight-fifteen be all right?"

"Perfect," I said. "I'll see you then."

Chapter Eight

Eight-fifteen. I had forty minutes, twenty of them traveling time. I ran upstairs, showered quickly, keeping my hair dry, washed my face, reapplied my makeup, and threw on a pale gray knit dress I never need to iron. Stockings, medium-height heels (I can't stand the high ones), earrings, my hair in a French twist. Done. It was ten to eight. I ran downstairs, threw on my coat, and was gone.

It was dark now, and a little colder, but the wind was barely perceptible. The air smelled like snow. I took Farwell to Ogden, and Jackson to Mason. The whole drive there I had the feeling I was going on a date. Just like a teenager—the same nervous anticipation, the old shyness resurfacing like one of those incurable viruses. It was ridiculous.

Karl Ratzsch's, on Mason Street, is a family-owned German restaurant known all over the country for its excellence in food, wine, and service. I've eaten there quite often, and enjoyed it every time. The decor is, well, sort of German, like you'd expect. Lots of steins, leaded-glass windows, antiques, hand-painted murals, and assorted ethnic paraphernalia. There's always a crowd, night or day, and often a bit of a wait, but it's well worth it, believe me.

I availed myself of the valet parking so I wouldn't have to trudge through any snow or slush in my inadequate shoes, gave my name to the maître d', and was directed to a gentleman in the bar, seated on a barstool with his back to me.

I went in and tapped him on the shoulder.

"Dr. Chapman?" I said.

101

He turned around, and gave me an engaging smile. I just about passed out, he was so gorgeous.

"Tony," he said, standing up and holding out his hand. "And I hope you're Beth." He had the same confident manner as his son—flirtatious, with no hint of shyness or self-doubt.

I laughed (and blushed, but fortunately the bar was so dark he couldn't see). "Yes, I am," I said, shaking his hand.

He had dark, wavy hair peppered with gray, a little thin on top but really attractive. Dark brows and lashes, dark eyes, and gleaming white teeth. He was tall, about six feet, athletically built—narrow hips, muscular legs, flat stomach, broad shoulders. He was wearing black jeans, a blue chambray shirt, and a blue tweed sportcoat. He looked an awful lot like Scott, only twenty-five years better, if you know what I mean.

He offered me his seat, which I declined, ordered me a champagne cocktail at my request, then turned around and looked at me.

"So," he said with a seductive smile, "do you always look this good on just a few minutes' notice?"

He was giving me an openly appraising look, but there was nothing leering about it, just frank appreciation. A little unnerving, but I loved it.

I shook my head and grinned.

Conversation was difficult because the bar was pretty noisy, but we managed to make small talk for fifteen minutes until we were shown to a table.

"Have you ever regretted leaving your firm?" he asked after the waiter had taken our drink order.

I smiled and shook my head. "No, I never have. I love what I do and I'm really happy being on my own. My hours are flexible if I want them to be, I'm my own boss, and I have control of my own life now. I don't think I could ever go back to the way things were before."

He gave me an approving look. "I know exactly what you mean," he said. "My father was a doctor, too. Cosmetic surgery. He'd always intended for me to take over his practice when he retired, join up with him right out of med school." He shook his head. "I just couldn't do it. I couldn't see spending my life that way. It wasn't me. It wasn't what I had in mind when I went to medical school. I may not have the income I might've had, but I'm doing something I really feel matters. So many of my patients are indigent, helpless. Some are even homeless. When I go home at night, I feel like I've accomplished something. I don't think I could've said that if I'd followed my dad's path.''

I smiled at him and nodded. ''Well, I think your son wants very much to follow your path,'' I said. ''He told me he hopes to practice with you someday.''

''He did?'' Tony said, a flush of pleasure sweeping across his face.

''Yes, he did,'' I said with a grin. ''He went on and on about how wonderful and dedicated you are and how badly you need his help. He says you had a partner who died?''

Tony winced. A mixture of pain and regret flickered in his eyes.

''Yes,'' he said. ''Art Freeman. He was a good man, a fine physician. Died of a heart attack at the age of forty-nine. He was cross-country skiing. They found his body frozen in the snow the next day. It was horrible. He had a wife and four children at home.''

He looked genuinely distressed at the memory, and I was sorry I'd brought it up. I didn't say anything. I didn't know what to say.

The waiter returned then and asked for our order. When he left, Tony looked at me with a serious face. ''You said you wanted to talk to me about Dave. I haven't let you do that. I apologize.''

''That's all right,'' I said. ''Believe me, I've been enjoying every minute of our conversation.''

He nodded graciously and smiled. ''So have I,'' he said. ''But now, please, what did you want to ask me?''

''Well, I'm not sure exactly. I'm trying to find out what was going on in his life before he died. So far, I've learned some pretty strange things but none of it makes any sense to me.''

Tony wrinkled his brow. "Like what, for instance, if you don't mind my asking?"

"Well, the bomb scares, for one. Did you know about that?"

He raised his brows. "Yes," he said. "Scott told me about that." He shook his head, a wry smile on his face. "Dave was far too intelligent to be doing something as reckless and stupid as that. I'll admit I was a little wild myself when I was that age, but I never pulled a stunt like that, not even close."

"He was also doing a lot of gambling, apparently."

Tony looked surprised, then laughed and shook his head. "Boy, did I misjudge him," he said.

"Now, I do have a question for you," I said, "but you don't have to answer this if you don't want to. I found a bankbook of his and it shows he deposited ten thousand dollars at the beginning of December, and I'm trying to find out where it came from. Did you pay him that much for the work he did for you, by any chance?"

Tony laughed. "I don't mean to laugh," he said. "But no. I paid him well, even more than he asked, but it was nowhere near that much. He only spent a total of maybe sixty hours on the project and he hadn't even completed it when he died."

"Had you paid him anything yet?"

"Yes. I paid him every week," Tony said. "I know what it's like being a college kid with no money coming in. I didn't think it'd be fair to make him wait until the end."

I nodded, and let out a long sigh.

"Maybe he won the money gambling," Tony said. "It might be as simple as that."

"Yeah, that's probably what it was," I said, although deep down I wasn't convinced.

"Did he ever talk to you about his personal life?" I asked.

"No, we didn't talk much about anything but what I hired him to do. That alone took more time than I'd anticipated, because I had a hard time describing what I wanted. I don't know the first thing about computers, unfortunately. I wanted to learn the basics and then have all my records put on a system so I could retrieve them at will. I thought it'd be a simple matter for him to set that up, but apparently I was mistaken.''

"How far did he get before he died?"

"I'm not even sure of that," Tony said with an embarrassed look. "I'm probably going to have to hire someone just to figure that out."

"Boy, that's too bad," I said. "Well, my brother does that sort of thing, so if you don't find anyone else, just let me know. I'm sure he could help you."

"Thanks," Tony said. "I'll keep that in mind."

"Did Dave ever receive any phone calls while he was at your office?" I asked.

Tony frowned, shaking his head. "Not that I know of," he said. "I was usually in with a patient, though, and he was there at night a few times after I'd already left. I just don't know."

"Did anyone come to see him?"

"Not that I'm aware of."

"How about his behavior?" I said. "Did he ever act strange, or out of the ordinary?

"I don't think so," Tony said. "But I wouldn't have had much of an opportunity to observe any change in his behavior. We didn't communicate much after the first few times. He usually came in and did his work and then left. I was either busy with a patient or at home."

I nodded, feeling a bit discouraged.

"Hey, it sounds like you're on the right track," Tony said. "At least you're coming up with questions. The answers will fall into place sooner or later."

I smiled appreciatively. "I hope so," I said.

He gave me a look of concern then. "I hope you're being careful," he said. "If he was murdered, there's someone out there with very little to lose. He may not balk at adding one more notch to his belt if he thinks you're getting too close to the truth."

"Well, thanks for worrying about me," I said with a smile, "but I'll be fine. Really."

Tony looked doubtful, and a little anxious, which I found kind of touching.

"Oh, I just thought of something else," I said. "Did you know anything about his medical condition?"

"What do you mean?" he said. "What medical condition?"

"His heart condition. The one he was taking the medication for."

"No, I wasn't aware he had a heart problem. It was an overdose that killed him, wasn't it?"

I nodded.

Tony shook his head. "Sorry," he said. "I can't help you there. He never mentioned it, and I don't know what heart medicine he was taking, if any. Did the police make any determination on that?"

"I have no idea," I said. "I've never even talked to them. As far as I know, they still think it's a suicide."

"Why are you so sure it wasn't a suicide?" Tony asked.

"A feeling, more than anything," I said. "And a lot of things just don't look right. For one thing, the suicide note didn't make any sense. It said he didn't want to face prosecution for the bomb scares, but they weren't going to prosecute him and he knew that."

Tony looked at me with interest. "I see," he said. "That does raise a few questions, doesn't it?"

The waiter approached, and asked if we'd like coffee or dessert. We ordered coffee, and took our time about leaving. I'd exhausted my mental list of questions and was tired of talking about it anyway. We spent the remainder of our time discussing my family and his, his divorce, mine. The usual sort of chitchat you engage in with someone you've just met.

When we walked outside, it was snowing lightly, soft flakes illuminated in the shafts of light beneath the street lamps. I'd enjoyed his company so much I didn't want to go home.

We ordered my car first. When he shook my hand as we were saying good-bye, he held on to it and looked into my eyes.

"It's been quite a while since I've relaxed like this," he said. "Thank you."

I smiled, and blushed, saved again by the lighting. "I enjoyed it, too," I said.

Tony gave the roof of my car a tap as I drove off.

Darn. Darn. Darn, I thought. This is all I need. Another man messing up my life. Well, I'd solve that problem. I just wouldn't think about him. At all.

When I woke up the next morning, it was still snowing. I turned on the radio and listened as I made my bed. Only three inches overnight and maybe another inch expected. Big deal. I took a shower, put on jeans and a sweater, and then looked out the window for Peter. Nowhere to be seen. Of course, it was only seven o'clock. What did I expect?

I went downstairs and made myself some Bisquick biscuits and a little pot of hot chocolate. Mmm. Snow food. This was the day I was to see Dr. King, and find out how Dave was most probably administered the overdose. But for now, I had work to do. I had a brief to get out that day and Emily had one due the next, so we'd all be busy, particularly Janice, poor thing. On days like this I feel guilty about not calling in a temp to help her, but what good would it do? I only have one computer. We try to anticipate overloads and I tend to get all my work done early, with several days to spare, but sometimes it just fails to work out the way I've planned. With all the investigating I'd been doing, I hadn't been keeping up with my regular schedule. Ordinarily, a brief due today would've been done last week, but this time I had a good third yet to be written. I didn't expect anyone until eight-thirty so I brought my file into the kitchen and worked while I ate.

The snow was still falling when I looked up an hour later, the flakes slightly larger than before. In case you haven't noticed, I love snow. I wasn't too fond of having to traipse through it when I was all dressed up and going into an office, but now that I'm on my own with nowhere I have to go, I thrive on it. I can just sit at my window and watch it fall.

Janice and Emily arrived at eight-thirty sharp, as promised, and went right to work. At twelve-thirty, we took a break, and lunched on cold chicken legs, a vegetable-pasta salad, and leftover biscuits.

At three, my brief was done and ready to go. I left the two of them working on Emily's and drove downtown to drop it off. Such door-to-door service isn't usually required, but this was an exception. The streets were clear, and it was no longer snowing, the air already turning colder as it so often does after a snow. I was back by four, leaving me about half an hour before I had to take off again to see Dr. King.

"Laura VanderHayden called while you were gone," Janice said. "She left a message on the machine."

"You have got to be kidding," I said. "I have been trying to get hold of her for days and every time I call, she's not there. Then I go out for a few minutes, and she calls while I'm gone. I can't believe this."

Janice and Emily stared at me, not saying a word.

"She said she'd be home all night," Janice said, the corners of her mouth turning up ever so slightly. "If you call her now I'm sure you'll catch her."

"Great," I said. I grabbed my "Dave" file, took it to the kitchen, found Laura's number, and dialed.

"VanderHayden residence," said a maidly voice.

I asked for Laura. She said she'd get her. A few minutes later, Laura answered the phone.

"This is Laura," she said.

"Laura, this is Beth Hartley," I said.

"Oh, I'm so glad you finally got me," she said in a barely audible voice. "I've been out of town for a few days. I'm sorry I wasn't able to get back to you sooner."

"That's okay," I said. "Are you free to talk?" Something about her voice told me she wasn't.

"Not on the phone," she said. "I really want to talk to you but it'll have to wait until I get back to Milwaukee."

"When are you coming back?" I said.

"Not until Saturday. I'm sorry. There's no way I can get away before then."

"What time are you getting in?"

"My flight is due to arrive a little before two," Laura said. "I could come and see you right after I get there if you want."

"That'd be great," I said. "Do you want me to pick you up at the airport?"

"Uh ... sure," she said. "I guess I hadn't thought about how I was going to get home."

We exchanged descriptions, agreeing to meet at the gate, and hung up. I'll have to admit, I was more than a little intrigued. She'd have to know something the others didn't. Of all the people in Dave's life, her connection to him was the most intimate.

I went upstairs, put on a burgundy corduroy skirt, matching opaque stockings, and a burgundy tweed fisherman sweater I made last year. There. Good enough for Dr. King. I told Janice and Emily to lock up if they left before I got back, and headed for the expressway.

Dr. King's office is on Oklahoma Avenue, right off of Sixtieth. I arrived a little before five-thirty, but the receptionist asked me to wait.

"Doctor is in with a patient. We were a little slow today. He had several emergencies this morning." She said this as if she took all emergencies in stride. Towering infernos, sudden deaths, losses of life and limb. She'd seen them all.

I sat in an orange molded plastic chair, one of many lined up against the waiting room wall. The walls were painted a sort of apricot color, accented with startling orange and fuschia chevrons that looked almost like they were darting from wall to wall. It was unsettling to look at. Probably even worse if you were sick.

I picked up a magazine from the table next to my chair, trying to avert my eyes. *Cosmopolitan.* I put it back. I picked up *Newsweek* next, and was in the middle of an article about Unified Europe, when she called my name.

"Doctor will see you now. It's the third door to your left," she said, pointing to the hallway beyond her cubicle.

Dr. King's door was open and he sat at his desk, making notes in a file. When he heard me approach, he looked up, smiled, and stood to shake my hand. His hand was sweaty, just as it had been the other day.

"Miss Hartley," he said. "It's good to see you. Please, have a seat. I'll be with you in a few moments."

I sat in one of the twin upholstered armchairs in front of his desk, and waited while he completed his notations. His office was nicely furnished, and decorated with taste, in sharp contrast to the waiting room. His desk was walnut, highly polished, his chair a luxurious black leather. The chair in which I sat, and the one next to it, were covered with an expensive-looking fabric the color of burgundy wine. The walls were gold, the rug an Oriental in varying shades of red, one of which matched the chairs perfectly. It was lovely. It didn't suit him at all.

He put his pen down on his desk with emphasis, closed the file the same way, and said, "There. Now what can I do for you?" He folded his hands and placed them in front of him on his desk. I guess I had his attention, huh?

I smiled, a little awkwardly, not really knowing what to make of him. He had a phoniness about him I didn't like. I always have trouble dealing with people like that. I don't know how to make conversation with them. I'm not sure how to respond to their comments.

"Well, I'd like to ask you a few questions about Dave's cause of death," I said. "I know you're busy. I promise to keep it short."

He waved at me dismissively, flashing me a disingenuous grin. "Don't give it a moment's thought," he said, looking at his watch. "My time is at your disposal. Now then, what can I tell you?"

"Can you tell me what kind of medication Dave was on and why he was taking it?" I said. I hoped he wouldn't cite doctor-patient confidentiality. After all, the patient was dead. He didn't care. Neither did his mom.

"Dave was taking a form of digitalis called digitoxin," Dr. King said. He pronounced the medical terms slowly and distinctly, in case I was too stupid to get it, I guess. Nice of him. Very thoughtful.

"Why was he taking the digitoxin?" I asked, enunciating the word in the same way he had. He lifted one brow just a teensy bit.

"Dave suffered recurrent episodes of rheumatic fever as a child which caused some damage to his heart. The digitoxin was part of the treatment for the damage."

"Was he using any other medications that you're aware of?" I asked.

"No, he was not," he said.

"Is there any way, that you can think of, that Dave could have been tricked into taking an overdose? Rather than being forced to do it, I mean."

Dr. King frowned. "What leads you to believe he was tricked?" he asked.

I shrugged. "Well, as far as I can tell, there wasn't any evidence of a struggle. Or forced entry, either. And it looks like he might have been planning to meet with the person who killed him."

Dr. King pursed his lips, and gave it some thought. "Well," he said, stroking his chin, drawing the whole thing out for effect. "How could he be induced to take the overdose without his knowing it?"

He tapped his upper lip with the index finger of his right hand, several times in succession, and nodded his head. "I suppose it could be done in any one of several different ways," he said. "The drug comes in two forms, tablet and liquid, and can be administered orally, intramuscularly, or intravenously." He defined both "intramuscular" and "intravenous" for me. What a guy.

"An injection, of course, he'd be aware of, but once it was given, a fait accompli. That's a French phrase meaning . . ."

"I know," I said. "How else?"

"It could be added to his food or to a beverage, as a liquid or a powder," he said. "Of course, the ingestion of food could have an impact on the absorption time, but it could be done." Dr. King nodded his head several times. "Yes, it could be done."

"How much would it take to kill him?" I asked.

"Well, that would vary with the individual, of course, depending upon body weight, medical condition, and use of other substances, but it wouldn't take much. Digitoxin is an extremely toxic drug. In Dave's case, it might require very little indeed."

"Why is that?" I said, frowning.

"Dave was a wrestler," he said. "He took it a bit too seriously, like many of these boys, and used laxatives to keep his weight down. Both his low weight and the laxative abuse would increase the risk of toxicity."

"So he could've been given a lethal dose in food or drink and not even have noticed it?"

"It's entirely possible," Dr. King said.

I nodded. "Okay," I said. "Thank you, Dr. King. That's all I wanted to know."

I stood and offered him my hand. He leaned forward from his chair, without actually rising to his feet, and took it.

"I hope I've been helpful," he said, looking as if he were sure he'd just provided me with case-cracking information.

"You have," I said with a smile. "Thank you very much for your time."

He got up then and walked me to the door.

"Feel free to call if you have any more questions," he said. I assured him that I would.

It was very cold when I left, and a brisk wind made it all the worse. I ran to my car, cranked up the heater, and sat in the lot until everything warmed up.

When I got home, I changed into sweatpants and a sweatshirt, made myself some pasta fajioli, and added some notes to my "Dave" file regarding my meeting with Dr. King. I did the same for Scott and Tony.

I went to the library after supper, curled up in my favorite chair, and read for a few hours. I did a little knitting for maybe half an hour, and went up to bed. Tony kept intruding upon my thoughts, but I pushed him away. Little good that did, he called the next day.

Chapter Nine

It was Wednesday, December thirtieth, a pretty uneventful day, all in all. Unlike the Wednesday after that, which I'm sure I'll never forget. Mrs. Gunther showed up early, whipped through the house like a madwoman, and was gone by two o'clock. She had to take Erma to her doctor's appointment.

Emily got her brief out, I sent Janice home early for a well-deserved rest, and Em and I got a head start on projects due in the next two weeks.

Then Tony called. My heart went flippety-flop and I patted myself on the chest.

"Hi," he said in a soft, almost caressing, voice. "How are you?"

"I'm fine," I said. "How are you?"

"Great. Listen, I only have a minute, but I have a question to ask you. I know this is disgustingly short notice, but are you doing anything New Year's Eve?"

"No," I said. "To tell you the truth, I usually stay home. I don't like the crowds."

"Neither do I," he said. "How would you like to have dinner with me, at my place? I'm a pretty fair cook, and I promise to be on my best behavior."

I took a deep breath. Oh, what the heck. "I'd love to," I said. "What time did you have in mind?"

"How about if I pick you up at eight?"

"Great," I said. "I'll look forward to it."

"So will I," he said.

I gave him directions to my house and hung up. This was not good. I was supposed to be forgetting all about this guy.

Emily left at six and I worked straight through until seven, had a bite to eat, and worked some more. Then I worked some more and went to bed.

The next day was Thursday, December thirty-first. I'd promised Janice and Emily short days but I got up early myself to make up for some of my lost time. They both arrived at eight-thirty, one right after the other, and left at three. When they were gone, I decided to knock off, too.

I had loads of time before Tony would be here and I was restless. I got out the "Dave" file and paged through every bit of it, making notes as I went.

I was stumped. I knew what killed him, and probably knew how it had been done. Chances were, it was someone he knew, someone he trusted enough to let in his apartment. And he might have arranged to meet him there, actually invited him over for some specific purpose.

But what?

He'd written *9:00* on his calendar, and hidden the calendar under a drawer. And the bankbook. Maybe he owed someone ten thousand dollars and meant to pay it back that night. Jake said he'd borrowed two thousand from "some guys" and hadn't paid them back. Maybe he'd borrowed more than Jake was aware of. But even if that were true, why would they kill him? If he paid up, they'd have no reason to complain. If he didn't, killing him wasn't going to get them anywhere.

And then there was the computer printout. I decided to call Jake and read some of it to him over the phone.

I dialed. Five rings, no answer. I was just about to hang up when I heard a breathless hello.

"Jake?"

"Yeah, who is this?"

"It's Beth," I said. "Are you all right?"

"Yeah, I just ran up the stairs. What's up?"

"Remember that computer printout I told you about? If I read some of it to you over the phone could you tell me if it means anything to you?"

"Sure," he said, "but make it quick. I gotta go."

"Okay," I said, and read him a few lines, after describing the format and telling him that each line was printed twice.

"Greek to me," he said. "Talk to you later." And he hung up.

I went through the list I'd made of people I intended to interview. I still hadn't talked to Dick Burghoff, but he'd probably be off to some party like Jake apparently was. I could try his wrestling coach, though.

I rooted through my notes for the number I'd gotten from the woman in the Computer Sciences office and dialed. A woman answered and I asked for Mr. Hodges.

"You just missed him," she said in a good-natured voice. "I just sent him to the store with a list. I can have him call you when he gets back."

"That'd be great," I said. I gave her my name and number and asked her to tell him I wanted to talk to him about Dave Grezinski. She said she would.

I sat for a while, thinking, then decided to try Dick Burghoff anyway. At the very least I could leave him a message. I dialed the number, and a young woman answered, almost in the middle of the first ring. I was immediately assaulted by raucous rock music and the sounds of a party in motion.

"Happy New Year!" she screamed into the phone. I yanked the receiver from my ear in a reflexive motion, and cautiously put it back.

"Is Dick Burghoff there?" I said in a loud voice.

"Hang on," she yelled.

Five minutes passed and nobody came to the phone. I hung up.

I went upstairs and looked through my closet, trying to decide what to wear that night. I didn't want to get too dressed up since I was only going to Tony's house, but I didn't want to underdo it, either. Oh, decisions, decisions.

I rejected the dresses, one by one, and settled on a navy velvet slacks and vest outfit I usually wear sometime during the holidays with an ivory organza blouse. I didn't need to press it so I just laid it out on the bed and went back downstairs.

I was making myself a cup of tea when Coach Hodges returned my call.

"Thank you for calling me back so soon," I said. I told him the whole story, including what I'd learned from Dr. King about the laxatives.

"Were you aware that he was using laxatives?" I said.

Coach Hodges hesitated briefly, before responding in a defensive tone. "None of my boys use that stuff," he said. "I strongly discourage it. It's unhealthy. There's no need for that."

I smiled, wondering how many of the others were doing the same thing as Dave.

"Did you know Dave very well?" I asked. "On a personal level?"

"There was a time I tried to get to know all my boys," he said. "Used to have 'em over to the house after meets, took 'em out after practice. None of 'em are interested anymore."

"That's too bad," I said, feeling sorry for him. "So you really didn't know anything about Dave's personal life?"

"Naw. Met his girl, once. Made a nice couple, I thought."

"Do you know if he hung around with any of the other wrestlers, other than Scott Chapman and Dick Burghoff?"

"Not that I ever saw," he said. "He did seem pretty tight with those two, though."

"Did you ever get the impression that anything was bothering him? Lately, I mean?"

He considered that for a moment. "Well, I'm not sure I'd say that," he said. "But he did mouth off more, seemed cockier somehow. They often do right around graduation, though. Probably nothing more than that."

"Well, thank you very much for talking to me, Mr. Hodges. If you think of anything else, would you call and let me know?"

"I sure will, little lady. Good-bye now."

I smiled when I hung up. He seemed like a nice man.

It was still early, so I NordicTracked for thirty minutes to dissipate some of my nervousness, had a piece of fruit, and read for a while.

At six-thirty, I showered and took my time getting ready to go. I hadn't realized how really anxious I was until then. I must have done my hair ten different ways before I was satisfied, my makeup three times. It was ridiculous.

I try so hard not to get attached to men, but it always happens when I least expect it. It's like they're waiting to ambush me, catching me off guard before I have time to put up my defenses. There was something about Tony I really liked, though. Okay, there was a lot about him I really liked. He was sensitive, caring, incredibly good-looking, divorced, uninvolved, charming in the most attractive way, and incredibly good-looking. Oh, I guess I mentioned that already.

On the other hand, he was involved with his work to the point of obsession, something he admitted played a major part in the demise of his marriage. He also avoided intimacy and commitment, he told me, fearing it wouldn't work out again, just like the first time. In that sense, we had a lot in common. I guess life's the only trip you go on where you're guaranteed *not* to lose your baggage, huh?

Tony arrived at eight, right on time (see, he's punctual, too), wearing dress slacks, a gorgeous cardigan sweater with a white Izod shirt, and a subtle after-shave that sent shivers up my body (the good kind).

"Hey, you look fantastic," he said, with his slow, lazy smile. "You really do."

"Thanks," I said, grinning. "So do you." It was so awfully corny.

"Great house," he said when I asked him inside. "The furniture is magnificent. Do you mind if I look around?" he said with a shy smile.

"No, not at all," I said. "Come on, I'll give you the full tour."

"I hope you don't mind my curiosity," he said as I showed him through the house, "but I collect antiques myself and you have some really fine pieces here."

"Oh, thanks," I said. I told him about Aunt Sarah, and how we'd shopped for many of them together.

We left then, drove no more than half a mile, and pulled

up in front of an absolutely gorgeous house with a slate roof and a turret on one side.

"What're we doing here?" I said.

Tony looked at me and grinned, and then turned off the ignition.

"You mean you live here?" I said.

He laughed. "I sure do," he said. "I couldn't believe it when you gave me your address. Come on. Now I can give you my tour."

The house was enormous, mansion-like in its proportions, and one I'd always admired from the outside. The interior was even better. There was a foyer with an inner door of leaded glass. The tile there and in the hallway beyond was the same black and ivory checkerboard sort I'd seen at Mrs. Grossman's, but Tony's was a lot less modern. The woodwork was dark, polished to a high gloss. Brass fixtures were everywhere.

The windows in the dining room and the living room were leaded glass. The dining room itself had dark wood paneling beneath a chair rail, fixtures and a chandelier beyond compare, several pieces of original art, and an awesome Oriental rug. The furniture was antique, as he'd promised. An eclectic assortment with more good taste, character, and charm than I think I've ever seen.

The turret had a winding staircase, with doors to the second and third floors. There were five bedrooms and four baths, each one unique, impeccably furnished and decorated. My own house seemed modest in comparison. I was speechless.

Tony laughed. "Well, what do you think?" he said.

I stared at him. "It's incredible," I said. "I've never seen anything like it. I absolutely love it."

He gave me a proud smile. "I hoped you would," he said. "Come on. I'll fix you a drink."

We went to the living room, where he settled me on the couch, and put a log on the fire he already had going. "What's your pleasure?" he said. "I have Scotch, champagne, wine, sherry, vermouth, whatever you like."

"How about champagne?" I said.

"Coming right up." He disappeared into the kitchen and

returned a few minutes later with a bottle of Dom Perignon and two champagne flutes. He filled both glasses, handed one to me, and raised his in a toast.

"To a happy new year, and many more," he said.

"Happy New Year," I said.

"I hope you're hungry," he said. "I probably made too much food but I sometimes get carried away."

"I'm always hungry," I said with a laugh. "Don't worry about a thing."

He put his glass down on the table in front of the couch and touched my knee with his right hand.

"Sit tight, then. I'll be right back."

He disappeared into the kitchen again, and returned several minutes later with a small tray of appetizers. Crab meat in little puff pastries, shrimp in a buttery garlic sauce, and assorted cheeses and smoked fish on flatbread and toast points. It was wonderful.

"Did you make these yourself?" I asked, unable to hide my amazement.

His cheeks tinted slightly and he shrugged. "It's a hobby of mine. I've always enjoyed cooking."

"Well, it shows," I said. "You're really good at it."

He smiled appreciatively and a little shyly, which made me like him all the more. Men. Such sneaky little devils, aren't they?

"How's your investigation going?" he asked. "Have you made any progress?"

I gave him a rueful smile. "No, not a bit," I said. "I talked to his cardiologist, though. That was kind of interesting."

"Who is he?" Tony asked.

"Thomas King. His office is in West Allis, on Sixtieth and Oklahoma."

He frowned for a moment, then shook his head. "No. Don't think I know him," he said. "What did he have to say?"

"He said Dave was taking digitoxin because he had rheumatic fever a lot when he was a kid."

Tony arched his eyebrows. "I didn't know that," he said. "So the cause of death was an overdose of digitoxin?"

I nodded. "He said it could've been put in his food or something he was drinking and he probably wouldn't even notice it."

"Interesting," Tony said.

"He also said it wouldn't take very much because Dave used laxatives to get his weight down for wrestling and that would make the digitoxin more toxic for some reason."

"Yes, that's true," Tony said, nodding. "I wasn't aware of his laxative abuse, either." He shook his head and exhaled sharply. "I guess I wasn't aware of a lot of things." He gave me a look tinged with pain and guilt.

"You can't blame yourself for that," I said. "You barely knew him. You only just met him a couple of months ago and you were busy with your practice almost every moment he was there."

Tony smiled appreciatively. "I know," he said. "I just can't help wishing I could have done something."

"Yeah, I know what you mean," I said. "I feel the same way and I never even met him."

Tony's dinner was salmon with a rich white sauce, new potatoes with butter and parsley, and fresh asparagus with hollandaise sauce. We had white wine, so good it didn't make me shudder, a chocolate mousse for dessert, then coffee and cognac by the fire.

He had candles on the table and he spent a lot of time watching me. His smile was subtly seductive, his come-on barely perceptible, but undeniably there. He asked me a lot of questions about myself and my family, and he listened intently as I talked. He'd move his eyes slowly across my face, paying particular attention to my eyes and mouth. His look was almost palpable.

At midnight, he kissed my hand and made me a toast I may never forget. We sat near the fire, listened to music, and talked some more, and at two, he drove me home.

He walked me to the door, and when I turned to say good night, he cupped the side of my face in his hand, and gently brushed my lips with his thumb.

"Good night, Beth," he said softly. And then he left. I could have killed him!

I hung up my coat, and walked into the library in a daze to check my messages.

I had one.

The voice was muffled and gravelly but the words were unmistakable:

"Mind your own business or you'll die."

I got into bed and turned out the lights, but I couldn't close my eyes. I stared in the direction of my bedroom door, which I'd closed, trying to adjust my eyes to the darkness so I could see the doorknob. I heard the furnace go on and then another noise and then my heart was beating so loudly I couldn't hear anything else. I took the telephone from the nightstand and put it under the covers with me. I had to go to the bathroom but I was afraid to get up. I was still wide awake when the sun started to rise, but I must have dozed off some time later. I didn't wake up again until eleven o'clock.

It was New Year's Day, a Friday, and I was expected at my parents' house. I was thoroughly grateful for that. I couldn't wait to get out of the house. I showered as quickly as I could, threw on some clothes, and headed straight for Wauwatosa without eating breakfast. I could do that at Mom's. I'd missed the brunch which she had planned for ten, and I had no idea how I was going to explain myself. My head hurt and I felt sick to my stomach. This private-eyeing was getting to be more than I'd bargained for.

I wanted to tell someone about it, just to calm myself down, but who could I tell? If I talked to Emily, she'd just say "I told you so." If I told Janice, she'd be scared out of her wits. Maybe I could talk to my dad. Or maybe not. I'd have to think about that. Boy, did I wish I'd called Brian McHenry when Emily had suggested it. Monday, first thing, I was going to do it.

"Sorry I'm late," I said to my mom when I walked into the kitchen.

She gave me a perplexed look. "Didn't you get my message?"

"What message?" I said.

"We're not eating until twelve. Ann and Don couldn't make it until then."

"Oh. Well, where are they?" I said. "It's quarter after twelve."

Mom looked at the clock, and tightened her jaw. "I'm putting this food on the table in five minutes," she said. "I could use some help." She was more than a little peeved, but it wasn't at me. Ha. Don and Ann to the rescue again.

We laid everything out, called Mike and my dad in from the den, and started eating. It was great. Bacon, sausage links, fried potatoes, scrambled eggs with onions and peppers, toast, blueberry muffins, coffee cake, and caramel-pecan buns. Don and Ann showed up at twelve-thirty, which wasn't too bad, and Mom was calmed down before the meal was over. No one even noticed I was a perfect wreck.

"What'd you end up getting off of that computer?" Mike asked me later when we were alone in the kitchen.

"Oh, nothing much," I said in a nonchalant voice. "The only files I printed were his monthly expenses and his medical bills. The rest of the stuff was just school projects and outlines or whatever."

Mike gave me a strange look. "What do you want with all that stuff anyway?" he said.

I shrugged, ready to give him some sort of fabricated response. Then I sighed and decided to just tell him the truth (except for the part about the threatening phone call, that is). He already knew something was up, anyway.

"You have to promise not to tell anyone," I said.

"Fine," he said. "Just tell me what's going on."

"All right," I said. "Remember when I told you Janice thought her brother had been murdered?"

"Yeah, so?" Mike said. He had a look on his face like he almost knew what was coming.

"Well," I said. "She asked me to help her prove it."

Mike gaped at me, a really annoying look on his face. "You're crazy!" he said.

"All I'm doing is trying to find out what was going on with him before he died. What's the big deal?"

"Don't you know how dangerous that could be?"

"I'm not going to do anything stupid," I said. "If I figure out who did it I'll just go to the police."

Mike looked somewhat relieved, but not entirely convinced.

"You might be able to help me, you know."

"I don't think so," he said. "I usually leave that sort of thing to the police."

"Just let me ask you one question, okay? It's about a computer printout I found in his desk."

Mike rolled his eyes and kept quiet. I took that as a yes.

"I'm just trying to figure out what it is," I said. "It's about a mile long and it has no title or anything. Maybe there never was one or maybe he just cut it off, I don't know. It actually looks like the top part was torn off."

Mike gave me a bored, and slightly impatient, look.

"It has three columns," I said. "None of them have headings, but the first one's a bunch of names, the second one has dates, and the third one's just numbers but they look like they could be dollar amounts. No dollar signs, though, so I'm not sure. Most of the numbers are the same. And then every name, date, and number is printed twice, one line right after the other. The dates go from January all the way through the end of November. Now, do you have any idea what it could be?"

He laughed. "How the heck should I know?" he said. "It could be anything. He could've retrieved data from some sort of records and just recorded it in that fashion. Maybe he was organizing it differently. Were the names in alphabetical order?"

"No, they were all over the place," I said. "But the dates were in order."

"Hmm. Well, I don't know. He was obviously organizing data of some sort and he was doing it by date. But you can see that for yourself."

"Why would he print every line twice like that?" I said.

"That I don't know. I don't know what purpose it'd serve. Unless he found it that way to begin with."

I frowned. "What do you mean?"

"Maybe the original source had everything entered twice."

I gave him an annoyed look. "Well, why would that be?"

"I don't know," Mike said. "You asked me what I thought and I'm telling you. I told you I don't know. I'm just trying to come up with possible explanations. What makes you think it's significant in the first place?"

"He hid it in a false bottom he made in his desk drawer."

Mike's eyes bugged out and he stared at me. "Are you serious?"

"Yeah. He also hid a calendar and a bankbook in the same place. The calendar had 'nine o'clock' written in for the night he died."

"Wow," Mike said.

"See what I mean? I think he hid that stuff for a reason, so the printout has to mean something."

"Yeah," he said. "Let me take a look at it sometime. Maybe something'll register if I see it."

"Okay," I said. "You want to do it tonight?"

He squinted. "How about tomorrow?"

"Fine," I said. "What time?"

"I don't know. I'll call you when I get up."

"Oh, I just remembered," I said. "His girlfriend's coming tomorrow. I'm picking her up at the airport at two so it'll either have to be in the morning or later in the afternoon after she leaves."

"I'll call you when I get up," he said.

"Okay. Oh, I just thought of something else," I said. "Dave was working for someone, putting all his business records on a computer, but he never finished it and he didn't teach the guy how to use it, either. Is it possible to just go in and look at something like that and figure out what he was doing?"

Mike wrinkled his brow. "You mean could I figure out the system and finish it for him?"

"Yeah."

He shrugged. "I'd have to see it, but sure, probably. Unless there was no indication of what he was doing."

"Well, I told the guy about you when he said he'd probably have to hire someone to finish it and he said he'd let me know."

"Fine. Whatever. Just have him give me a call."

"Okay," I said. "Now don't forget. Don't tell anyone about this. Promise?"

Mike rolled his eyes again. "Don't worry about it," he said. "I'll call you tomorrow." And he walked out of the room.

The rest of the day was pretty enjoyable. The guys watched football all day, the kids hardly even fought, and Ann and I got along reasonably well. Something had to be wrong, but I wasn't going to complain. We had another meal at five—baked ham, twice-baked potatoes, some green bean dish my sister always makes with onion rings on top, and cranberry-apple cake for dessert. Ann and Don went home at seven, Mike at eight. At nine, I finally got up the nerve and left, too, still fearful of going back in my house.

I put the car away, unlocked the door with my heart pounding in my throat, and ran through the house turning on all the lights. The sheer size of the place had been unsettling when I'd first moved in. So many rooms, and so much space. I'd keep imagining I heard someone in another part of the house. It'd taken months to get over that, and now it was back, bigger and stronger than ever. The worst part is the basement; I'm always wondering if someone is down there. The only comfort is in knowing they can't enter through a basement window. They're too narrow for anyone but a small child to fit through.

Should I go down there, or not? If I did, I'd probably faint from fright. If I didn't, I wouldn't sleep all night. I decided to take my chances and get it over with.

I put my hand on the mudroom door, yanked it open, and switched on the light. Empty. Now I had to go through the same thing with the basement door. I put my ear to the door first, and listened. Nothing—at least I was pretty sure I heard nothing. I put my hand on the knob, my heart beating wildly. I turned the knob slowly, and pulled the door open. No one at the top of the stairs. I turned on the basement light. I tiptoed down the stairs, pausing at every step to listen. No one, nothing.

I turned the lights on at the bottom of the stairs and whipped my head around the corner. There was no one in the room, unless they were in the powder room or the shower. I started toward the shower and changed my mind. I'd do the shower and the powder room last. I went to the doorway between the two main rooms, reached my hand around the corner, and switched on the lights.

This room wasn't as easy to search. There are a lot of corners to peek around because of the way the place is configured. I approached the furnace, took a deep breath, and quickly looked behind it. I did the same with the other hidden spots. Nothing. No one there. Okay. The only places left to look were the shower and powder room.

I went back to the first room, hesitated more than a few moments, and threw back the shower curtain. It was empty. Now for the powder room. I held my breath, put my hand on the knob, turned it slowly, yanked the door open—and screamed! My own reflection had just scared me half to death. I'd always dreaded the day that would happen but I didn't think I'd be so young.

I turned out the lights, made sure every door was bolted, and went up to bed. I lay there for a good half-hour, my heart still beating like a drum, and tried to come up with a way to get this over with so I could feel safe again. I couldn't think of a thing.

Chapter Ten

When I woke up the next day, there was frost on my windows, delicate little portraits of fairies and mountains and lace. It was twenty below zero with a windchill of negative thirty. I had some shredded wheat and a mango for breakfast, made a pot of tea, and read through some cases Em had copied for me at the law library.

Mike called at eleven and said he couldn't make it before I went to the airport. Maybe later in the afternoon. He'd let me know.

I worked straight through until one, had a bowl of soup, and left to pick up Laura. I got there with ten minutes to spare, parked, and checked the monitor to see if her flight was on time. It was ten minutes late. Not too bad.

I walked to the Northwest terminal, found a seat at the gate, and watched the people go by. I never get bored in an airport. I just look at the people and try to guess where they're going and where they're from. The good-looking ones are all from Milwaukee, of course.

The plane pulled in fifteen minutes late. A young woman with long brown hair, brown eyes, no makeup, wearing jeans with holes in the knees and boots that looked like a construction worker's, walked off alone carrying a knapsack and a down jacket over her shoulder. She was about Emily's height and weight, and she fit the description Laura had given me. She also looked an awful lot like the woman in the pictures I'd seen on Dave's bulletin board. She looked around as if she were searching for someone, and rested her gaze on me. I got up and walked toward her.

"Are you Laura?" I asked.

"Yes," she said, smiling. "Are you Beth?"

I nodded. "I'm sorry you had to wait," she said. "We took off late."

"That's all right," I said. "Do you have any luggage?"

"Yeah, about a thousand bags. I got a new set for Christmas and I filled them with all the other stuff I got. My dad really went berserk this year. I think he was trying to make up for Dave."

I smiled. "Well, it's nice to know he cares," I said.

She gave me a look like I was the most naïve person in the world.

We spent almost forty minutes retrieving her luggage, piled it all on a rent-a-cart, and tried to pull it to the parking lot. We'd get it about two feet and something would fall off. After the third such mishap, I told her to wait where she was, went back and got a second cart, and put half on that.

We loaded everything in the car, which wasn't easy, paid more money to get out than I thought I should have to, and headed downtown.

"You know, maybe I should just take you home first, at least to drop off your luggage," I said. "In fact, if you want, we could talk there, although, in that case, we'd have to stop at my house first. I want to ask you about something I found in Dave's apartment and I don't have it with me."

Laura hesitated. "No, that's too much trouble," she said. "Let's just go to your place. I don't mind leaving the stuff in the car, if you wouldn't mind taking me home later."

"Oh, no, of course not," I said. "I was planning to do that."

"This is a great street," Laura said as I unlocked my front door. "I've never been here before."

"Thanks," I said with a grin. "It's my favorite in the whole city. My Aunt Sarah left the house to me. Sometimes I feel like I'm living a fairy tale."

She gave me a funny look.

"Wow!" she said when she walked through the foyer. "This is so cool."

I could see by her face that she was sincerely impressed, which amazed me no end. Wasn't she the one with the maids and the butlers, chauffeurs, and ladies-in-waiting?

"I love your antiques," she said. "Gosh, you have the greatest taste."

I laughed. "Thanks," I said. She made no attempt to disguise her enthusiasm, just walked right in and started checking things out. I liked her. I'd been expecting snobbery, maybe cashmere and pearls, I don't know.

"Do you have time for a tour?" I said.

"Sure," she said. "How many rooms do you have?"

I opened my mouth, and shut it again. "I don't know," I said. "I never counted them. Seven bedrooms and four-and-a-half baths, but I don't know how many altogether."

I took her through the whole house and watched her inspect my furnishings as if she were appraising them for an insurance policy.

"I love antiques," she told me. "My mom collects them, too. She usually waits till I'm home to go hunting 'cause I have a fit if she goes without me. We hit all the auctions and estate sales. Are you into that?"

"Actually, I've never even been to an auction," I said. "I used to go to estate sales with my mom and my aunt, sometimes, but we usually just shopped in antique stores."

She nodded.

"I always felt weird at estate sales," I said. "Like I was intruding on someone's privacy or something."

Laura wrinkled her brow. "Yeah, I kind of know what you mean," she said. "I just never thought of it like that."

"Are you hungry?" I said when we'd completed the circuit.

She hesitated, then shrugged. "Yeah, I could eat something. All they had on the plane was some really gross powdered egg thing."

I winced. "You should fly Midwestern next time. Their food is great."

She looked skeptical.

"I'm serious," I said. "I actually look forward to it."

We went into the kitchen where I offered Laura a seat and gave her several choices for lunch. She opted for a cheese sandwich and a Coke, so I made the same for both of us.

"Have you lived in Boston all your life?" I asked her as I was making the sandwiches.

"Yeah, it's pretty cool. You ever been there?"

"Twice," I said. "I love it. It's a great city. I actually went on one of my honeymoons there."

She frowned. "You went on more than one honeymoon?"

"Well, only one with each husband," I said.

She raised her eyebrows.

"Are you planning to move back after you graduate?" I asked.

She hesitated, a touch of sadness flickering across her face. "Yeah, I guess I will now," she said.

I finished the sandwiches and we made small talk while we ate, primarily because I was stalling, feeling unsure how to open the topic. I really hated to bring up Dave's death—even worse, his life—forcing her to relive all the horror and pain she must have experienced in the last few weeks. Fortunately, she eased me into it herself.

"What was that thing you wanted to show me?" she said when we'd finished eating.

"Oh, just a minute," I said. "I'll go get it."

I went to the library, retrieved my whole "Dave" file, and came back.

"I found this in his desk, hidden under a drawer," I said, handing her the printout. "No one seems to have any idea what it is. Does it mean anything to you?"

She looked at it, leafing through a half-dozen pages, and wrinkled her brow. "I've never seen it before," she said. "Maybe it was for school."

I raised my eyebrows and made a face. "Well, we'll probably never know." I put it away.

Then I showed her the calendar notations. "Do you have any idea what he was doing at nine o'clock that night?"

She shook her head. "No, I don't think he said. He took

me to the airport on Thursday and I talked to him on the phone after I got home but I don't remember him saying anything about Friday.''

I nodded. "Okay," I said. I showed her the bankbook transactions next. She didn't even react.

"Did you know he had this much money?" I said.

"I don't know, I guess."

"Do you know where he might have gotten it?"

"He could've gotten it lots of places. Gambling, work, whatever. He did lots of things for people for money."

I frowned. "Like what?" I said.

Laura sighed. "Well, I suppose you know about the bomb scares."

I stared at her with wide eyes. "Are you telling me someone actually paid him to do that?"

"Yeah," she said with a shrug. "Some guy offered him five hundred bucks to do it so he did."

"Do you know who the guy was?" I asked.

She shook her head. "Just some guy he met at the bars."

"Did Dave tell you why the guy wanted him to do it?"

"The guy never told *Dave*," Laura said. "It was kind of stupid, really. I don't think he should've done it."

I shook my head. This was too much. "Do you know if the guy ever paid him?" I said.

"I don't know. Probably."

I wrinkled my brow, something suddenly occurring to me. "Why would some guy he'd never even met before ask him to do something like that? It doesn't make sense."

"He was a friend of someone who knew Dave and the guy told him Dave would do anything for money, which was true."

"I just can't believe this," I said.

Laura shrugged, again. None of what she was telling me seemed to strike her as unusual. It was as if she thought this was all normal, everyday stuff.

"Do you know if he borrowed money from anyone?" I asked.

"I don't see why he'd have to borrow money," she said.

"He obviously had enough of his own." She looked at me as if I were a bit obtuse.

I'd made a list of things I wanted to ask her, so I took it out and looked at it, checking off the things I'd already covered.

"Do you want anything else to drink?" I said. "Another Coke or coffee or anything?"

"I'll have another Coke," she said. "Thanks."

I went to the refrigerator, and refilled both our glasses. "You want anything else to eat?" I said. "I have cookies, or ice cream?"

She smiled. "No, this is fine," she said. "Thanks."

I looked at her for a few moments. "I almost hate to ask this," I said, "but why weren't you at the funeral?"

She colored slightly, and lowered her eyes. "My dad wouldn't let me," she said through clenched teeth.

"Jake said your dad wasn't too happy about your seeing Dave," I said.

"That's putting it mildly," Laura said. "My dad hated Dave. He didn't want me to have anything to do with him. He never even gave him a chance. He just wrote him off the minute he saw him."

"When did he meet him?"

"Thanksgiving. I brought him home with me so he could meet my family. I gave him this big buildup like they were really great, you know? And my dad just treated him like dirt. I thought I was going to die. I was never so embarrassed in my life."

I gave her a sympathetic look. "Why did your dad dislike him so much?"

Laura shook her head, and her eyes filled with tears. "I don't know," she said. "He just hated him right away. You could just see it. He's such a jerk, you wouldn't believe."

She was sniffling, and wiping the tears from her cheeks with the back of her hand. I got up and found her some tissues.

"I'm sorry," she said after she'd blown her nose and dried her face.

"You don't have to be sorry," I said. "I think you have some pretty good reasons to cry."

She laughed and sobbed at the same time, and blew her nose again.

"Did your dad know you were still seeing Dave?" I said.

Laura shook her head. "No, I told him I broke up with him. He threatened to cause Dave a lot of trouble if I didn't."

I frowned. "What kind of trouble?"

Laura gave me a jaded look. "Who knows?" she said. "There's no end to what my dad can think up to ruin people's lives. He's a politician."

I started to smile, but caught myself.

"How'd you find out about Dave's death?" I asked.

"A friend of mine called me. She read about it in the paper."

"Have the police talked to you yet?"

"Yeah," she said. "I'm supposed to go down there later. They want to talk to me in person."

I nodded. "Well, tell them everything you told me," I said. "The more they know, the easier it'll be for them to find this guy." She didn't respond, just stared out the window.

"What were you going to do about getting married?" I said a few moments later.

"Do it behind my dad's back," Laura said. "Ignore him. I hate him. He said he'd disinherit me if I married Dave but I didn't care. I don't want his lousy money."

"Are you the only child?" I asked.

She nodded. "Yeah. I suppose that's why he's so protective. That's what Dave said, anyway."

"How about your mom? What did she think about it?"

Laura snorted. "My mom doesn't think, she just does whatever my dad tells her. All he has to do is look at her and she's trembling in her boots. Sometimes I just want to tell her to wise up and get a life."

I smiled weakly, not really knowing what to say.

"Did you know any of his friends?" I said. "Besides Jake and Scott Chapman and Dick Burghoff?"

She shook her head. "Not really, not that I could name."

I nodded. I looked over my list of questions, again. I'd covered everything on it, and I really couldn't think of anything else to add. "Would you like anything else to drink?" I said.

"No," she said without energy. "Would you mind taking me home now? I'm really tired and I still have to go to the police station."

I smiled. "Sure," I said. "Come on."

I drove Laura home, helped her carry her luggage inside, exchanged phone numbers with her, and left. It was five o'clock. Mike hadn't called and I just remembered I'd promised to call Mrs. Robinson about our visit the next day. I was really looking forward to that. Maybe I could cook something and bring it along.

I dialed Mrs. Robinson's number as soon as I hung up my coat. I let it ring for quite a while, knowing it might take her some time to get to it. She answered on the tenth ring, sounding quite out of breath.

"Hello?" she said.

"Mrs. Robinson, this is Beth Hartley," I said. "Do you remember me from last Sunday?"

"Oh, Beth," she said in a delighted voice. "Oh, my dear. I should say I do. How are you getting along?"

"I'm fine," I said. "How are you? Are you keeping your door locked?"

"Yes, I am," she said. "I kept my promise."

"It's only until the killer's caught," I said. "I'm sure it'll be all right to keep it open again after that."

"Oh, I hope so," she said. "Now, then, are you calling about our visit tomorrow?"

"Yes, I am," I said. "I was thinking maybe I could cook something for us and bring it over. Would you like that?"

"That would be lovely," she said.

"What's your favorite thing to eat?" I said.

She laughed. "Well, now, I don't know. Let me give that some thought. My favorite thing to eat. Hmm. Let me see."

True to her word, she did give it some thought, for almost three minutes.

"Pork chops," she said decisively. "Pork chops and corn."

"Pork chops and corn it is," I said. "What time would you like me to come over?"

"Oh, my. Anytime," she said. "I don't have any plans but to see you."

"Well, what time do you usually eat supper?" I asked.

"Oh, five or thereabouts."

"Okay," I said, "then how about if I get there at four? That'll give us time to talk before dinner and I can heat everything up in your oven. How's that?"

"That's super," she said. Super. I couldn't believe it. She was so cute.

I hung up, and decided to call Mike. It was after six and I hadn't heard from him. He was home, but on his way out, and he apologized for not getting back to me.

"How about tomorrow?" he said.

"That'll be fine as long as it's in the morning," I said. "I have to do some cooking and baking in the afternoon and be somewhere by four."

"Okay," he said. "That's fine. I'll call you."

I rolled my eyes. "Okay. Talk to you tomorrow," I said.

I spent the rest of the night knitting and reading, and went to bed at ten o'clock.

I woke up at nine the next morning, made myself an omelette and some toast for breakfast, and went grocery shopping to get the things I needed for my dinner with Mrs. Robinson. I decided to make biscuits to go with the pork chops and corn, and an apple pie for dessert. I found everything I needed, including cinnamon ice cream to go with the pie.

Mike hadn't called by the time I got home, so I made the pie and baked the pork chops in gravy. The biscuits I'd make at the last minute. The corn I could heat at her house.

Mike called at eleven-thirty.

"Sorry," he said, sounding flustered. "Is it too late for me to stop by?"

"No," I said. "I already did most of what I had to do, so it's fine."

"Good," he said. "How about if I swing by in a few minutes? I can't stay long, though. I have to be somewhere."

"That's okay," I said. "It won't take very long."

I hung up, made a pot of tea, and poured myself a cup. Mike was here ten minutes later (he lives only a few miles away) and I handed him the printout. He paged through it quickly, but carefully, his eyes darting across the page as he read line after line. After about five minutes of that he put it down.

I raised my brows. "Well?" I said.

"It could be a record of office billings of some kind. Medical possibly. Didn't you say he was working for a doctor?"

I frowned. "Well, yeah, but . . ."

He shrugged. "Find the guy and ask him."

I nodded, and stared out the window. "Yeah, I guess I could do that."

"I have to get going," Mike said. "Is that all you wanted to show me?"

"Yeah, that's it," I said.

"Okay. Catch you later," he said. And he was gone.

I was disturbed. I didn't like this. I didn't want to think that Tony figured in this at all, even tangentially. I sat at the table, nervously doodling in the margins of the printout, drinking cup after cup of tea. I was going to be a complete wreck until I found out, I decided, so I called him.

"Hi, it's Beth," I said when he picked up the phone.

"Well, hey, what a pleasant surprise," Tony said. "I was just thinking about you."

I smiled, a wash of desire and anxiety colliding to form a knot in the pit of my stomach.

"I have to ask you something," I said, just to get it over with.

"Sure," he said. "What's up?"

"I found a computer printout in Dave's apartment and I showed it to my brother Mike and he says he thinks it might be some sort of medical billing record. It's just a bunch of names and dates and numbers that look like they could be dollar amounts. If I read some of them to you do you think you'd be able to tell if it was something he might've been doing for you?''

''I don't know,'' Tony said with a laugh. ''We can give it a try.''

I read about ten names with the corresponding dates and numbers and then he stopped me.

''I don't recognize any of those names,'' he said. ''And the numbers wouldn't be right. I'm sure it wasn't anything he was doing for me.''

I let out an enormous sigh. ''Thanks,'' I said. ''That's all I wanted to know.''

He laughed. ''Sorry I couldn't help you.''

''Don't be sorry,'' I said. ''I just had to ask.''

''I had a great time Thursday night,'' he said.

''So did I,'' I said. ''You're a great cook.''

''I hope that wasn't all you enjoyed,'' he said with a mock-wounded tone.

I laughed. ''No, believe me, it wasn't.''

''Well,'' he said, ''I hate to cut this short, but I'm due at Scott's in ten minutes and I'm already running late. Can I call you later in the week?''

''Sure,'' I said with a grin.

I pulled up in front of the apartment building at ten minutes to four, and carried everything up to Mrs. Robinson's in two trips. The second time up, I ran into Gordon Kohn in the hall.

''Oh, hi,'' I said. ''How are you?''

He took a moment, then a flash of recognition crossed his face.

''Beth, right?''

I nodded.

''I'm fine, how're you?'' he said. ''Are you making any progress on the case?''

I shrugged, giving him a sheepish smile. ''A little,'' I said. ''I'm getting there, but it's pretty slow going.''

He grinned, put a key in his door, and unlocked it. ''Hang

in there,'' he said. He walked into his apartment and closed the door.

"I can hardly wait to eat this scrumptious dinner," Mrs. Robinson said, giving me a hug. "I can see you've gone to quite a bit of trouble on my account."

"It wasn't any trouble at all," I said with a smile. "I enjoyed making it and I'm going to enjoy eating it with you even more."

She grinned happily, clearly delighted to have me there. I felt a surge of emotion, almost to the point of tears. I'd become so fond of her in so short a time, I could barely believe it.

"Now sit down on the sofa with me and tell me all about your week," she said. She patted the seat right beside her and I took it obediently. "How is your investigation progressing?" she asked in a conspiratorial voice.

I smiled. "Not very well, I'm afraid. I've found out a lot more but I still can't figure out who did it. It could be so many people."

"Well, I have faith in you, my dear. If anyone can crack this case, you can."

I grinned and squeezed her arm. We talked for another forty minutes about this and that, and then I got up to take care of the dinner. I'd already put the pork chops in the oven on low. I raised the temperature, put the corn on, and set the table. Fifteen minutes later, dinner was ready, the biscuits nice and hot, and the pork chops heated through but still tender and moist because of the gravy. I'll have to admit, the meal was really good. Mrs. Robinson thought so, too.

"My dear, these are the tastiest pork chops I've ever eaten," she said. "And the *biscuits*. They're heavenly."

I grinned, feeling quite proud of myself.

"Have you seen Mrs. Markham lately?" I asked her.

"Yes," Mrs. Robinson said. "She stopped by today, as a matter of fact. She told me she had a nice chat with you last week."

I smiled. "She was nice," I said. "I talked to her for quite a while. I also went to see Gordon Kohn in apartment 316."

"Oh, yes, he came to see me the other day. Just wanted to look in on me to see how I was doing, he said. Now wasn't that thoughtful of him?"

I hesitated before I smiled. "Yes, it was," I said.

When we'd finished dinner, I put the pie in the oven to warm, and made a pot of tea. Mrs. Robinson made an even greater fuss over the dessert than she had the dinner. I'll tell you, if everyone was that appreciative, I'd cook for people all the time.

I stayed for another hour, and then she looked tired, so I decided it was time to leave. I packed everything up, gave her a big hug and kiss, happily accepted several minutes more of praise and gratitude, and promised I'd call her next week.

After she bolted herself in, I considered knocking on the doors of the tenants I'd been unable to talk to the week before, but decided against it. They'd probably be a lot more receptive if I didn't bother them on a Sunday night. It was time I went home anyway. I'd spend a leisurely hour reading, get to bed a little early, and call Brian McHenry as soon as I got up.

Chapter Eleven

I called the police administration building first thing Monday morning, before Janice, Emily, and Mrs. Gunther arrived, and left a message for Brian McHenry.

Janice showed up early, at twenty to nine, so I took advantage of the time to tell her about the latest developments.

"Somebody *paid* him to do that?" she screeched. "Who?"

"She doesn't know," I said. "Just some guy he met through someone else."

Janice's face turned a bright pink and she looked away, shaking her head in disbelief.

"They really were planning to get married, by the way, but it was because of Laura's father that they were keeping it a secret. For some reason, he was totally against it. He didn't want her seeing him at all."

"Who does he think he is?" Janice said.

"I don't know," I said. "Some hotshot senator from Boston. Probably used to getting his own way, you know?"

Janice turned down her mouth in disgust.

Emily came in then, poured herself a cup of coffee, and sat down at the table. Mrs. Gunther arrived a few minutes later, took one look at us sitting in the kitchen and scampered toward the library.

"I'm going to vacuum that room while I have the chance," she said over her shoulder.

I gave Mrs. Gunther the time she needed, then the three of us got down to work. At eleven-thirty, Brian McHenry returned my call. I took it in the kitchen, so I could talk freely, and brought my "Dave" file with me.

"Hey, is this the same Beth Hartley I pined away for through eight long years of grade school?" he said.

I laughed. "This is the first I ever heard of that."

"Well, I was shy back then," Brian said. "You know how it is."

I laughed again, mostly out of nervousness. I was feeling a little uneasy and strange, talking to someone whose voice I hadn't heard for thirty years, whose face I hadn't seen since the eighth grade.

"How did you know where to find me?" he asked.

"Emily Schaeffer," I said. "She suggested I call you."

Brian hesitated a moment. "How is Emily?" he said in an odd voice.

I told him she was fine, happily married, and even more happily working for me.

"That's great," he said. "Say hello for me."

"I will."

"So, what can I do for you?" he said. "I have a feeling this isn't just a social call."

I took a deep breath and let it out. "No, it isn't," I said. "I called you because Emily told me you were a homicide detective and I'm kind of involved in a homicide right now."

"Is that right?" he said in a cautious voice.

"Well, I'm not involved exactly. I'm just investigating it."

"You're investigating a homicide," Brian said flatly. "Maybe you'd better tell me about it."

So I did. I told him about Dave, Janice asking me to help, a skeletal outline of what I'd done so far, and the message I'd found on my answering machine.

"Hold on," he said. He cupped his hand over the phone and yelled something to someone, but I couldn't make out what.

"Tell me what the message was, exactly," he said.

" 'Mind your own business or you'll die.' That was it."

"Man, woman?"

"Man," I said. "At least I think it was a man. The voice was kind of weird."

"How so?"

"I don't know. Kind of muffled. And funny. Like he was trying to disguise it."

"Did it sound familiar?" Brian said.

"No, I don't think so."

"Okay. You saved it, didn't you?"

I didn't say anything.

"You did save it, didn't you?"

"I meant to but I erased it by mistake. I'm sorry," I said.

I heard Brian groan. "All right," he said. "Don't worry about it. Okay. This isn't my case. It belongs to a guy named Bruce Cousins. What I ought to do is have you come down and talk to him directly, but I'd rather talk to you myself. How about going to lunch with me? Are you free?"

"Sure," I said. "When and where?"

"Where are you now?"

I told him.

He thought for a moment. "I'm at Seventh and State so how about meeting me at the Pfister?" he said. "In the coffee shop?"

"That'd be fine," I said. "What time?"

"Twelve-thirty?"

"Okay. See you then."

"Beth?" Brian said as I was about to hang up.

"Yes?"

"Meet me in the lobby. It'll be easier to find each other that way."

"Okay," I said. "I'll see you in an hour."

I hung up with a grin. I couldn't wait. This was somebody I hadn't seen in thirty years. *Thirty years.* For some reason, I found that absolutely amazing.

What in the world should I wear?

I ran upstairs, pulled a half-dozen skirts from my closet, stared at them, and went back for more. I tried on two dresses, three skirts with about a hundred different combinations of sweaters and blouses, and a turquoise tweed wool jumper. I decided on the jumper with a light gray sweater underneath, threw it on, fixed my makeup (twice), redid my hair (three times), and finally rushed out the door, leaving a huge pile of clothes on the bed.

The Pfister Hotel is on Wisconsin Avenue, a few blocks east of the river. I absolutely love it. It's the oldest hotel in the city, and it has three restaurants, all very nice (especially the English Room which, quite honestly, is superb). The coffee shop is the most casual, although it's a little fancier than it used to be. The food is really good now, but I kind of miss the old place.

I was there a little early so I sat on one of the lobby chairs and watched the people go by. The lobby is just gorgeous. It has a marble staircase with two bronze lions at the bottom. It's such an elegant, sort of old-fashioned place. Someday I'm going to rent a room there and stay for a few days, just for fun.

I didn't recognize Brian at all when he walked over. He was very tall, well-built, with wire-rimmed glasses, light brown, slightly wavy hair, cut short in a traditional man's style. He was wearing a suit, gray tweed, with a white shirt and striped tie, wing tips, and a trench coat. He looked great. I couldn't believe it was him.

"Beth Hartley?" he said when he approached.

"Brian?" I said, showing my surprise.

"Wow, you haven't changed at all. You look exactly the same," he said.

I wrinkled up my face. "Brian, that's impossible."

"Well, okay," he said with a sheepish grin. "Not exactly. But I knew it was you. I recognized you as soon as I saw you."

I laughed, and stood up.

"You're still the same height," he said.

"Thanks a lot, Brian. I guess I can't say the same for you, though."

"Tell me about it," he said with a laugh. "I shot up six inches my first year of high school."

"Good grief," I said. "Could you feel it?"

"No," he said, eyeing me curiously. "Are you hungry?"

"Always am," I said.

He was staring at me. "You look great," he said. "Really great."

"Thanks," I said, blushing. "So do you." Boy, this was awkward. I was glad I had a murder to talk about.

"So," Brian said after we'd ordered, "what have you been doing all these years?"

I told him about law school, the firm, my business. How I happened to hire Emily. My house. My marriages. All that sort of thing. He told me about his divorce (no kids either), his career, his lack of a social life. We talked for over an hour, just about personal things, but then he got serious.

"I want to talk about the Grezinski case," he said.

I took a breath, feeling like I'd just been called to the principal's office.

"I want you to start at the beginning, tell me everything you know, everything you've done, people you've talked to, et cetera, et cetera. Okay?"

"Okay," I said.

"Start with how you got involved to begin with." He leaned back in the booth, stretched his right arm across the back, and waited.

"Well," I said, "his sister Janice is my secretary and we're pretty close. I've known her for over ten years. She was the one who found his body. Well, she wasn't the only one, but I'll get to that later."

Brian raised one eyebrow but remained silent.

"She was supposed to go out to breakfast with him on the day after he died but he never showed up so she went over to his apartment and she found him. He was lying on the floor with an empty pill bottle in his hands and there was a suicide note in the typewriter. It wasn't his room or his typewriter, by the way—it was Jake's, which is weird in itself."

Brian sat forward. "Wait a minute. Who's Jake?"

"Dave's roommate. He's the other one who found the body."

Brian pulled a pad and a pen from his pocket. "Give me his full name," he said.

I did.

"Address, phone number?"

I did. "He's already talked to the police," I said.

"When did he find the body?"

"Friday night," I said. "But you're getting me off track now. I'll get to that."

The corners of Brian's mouth turned up a little and he leaned back again.

"Anyway," I said. "He's lying on the floor with this pill bottle which is a prescription for the heart medication he took, digitoxin, and there's a note in the typewriter. Only the note didn't make any sense, according to Janice."

"How so?" Brian said.

"Well, first of all, it said he couldn't pay his debts and Janice didn't think he had any debts, although it looks like she might've been wrong about that. But the other thing was, it said he didn't want to face prosecution for those bomb scares they had at Marquette during finals. He was the one who did that. But they weren't going to prosecute him and he knew that so he couldn't have written the note. You see what I mean?"

Brian took off his glasses and rubbed his eyes. "I think so. Go on."

"So she asked me to help her prove he was murdered."

"And you said yes, just like that."

"Yes, I did."

He stared at me for almost a minute, with a really strange look on his face. I was getting ready to strangle him.

"What did you do then?" he said finally.

I told Brian a sort of truncated version of everything that had transpired so far. He seemed particularly interested in Jake and Laura.

"Neither one of them showed up at the funeral?" he said.

"No, but Laura's dad wouldn't let her go. He didn't want her to have anything to do with Dave and I guess it applied even after he was dead."

Brian made a few notes. I was trying to see what he was writing, but he was shielding it from my view. You know, I'll have to admit, that really annoyed me.

"Do you know any more about that?" he asked. "Did her father ever make any threats?"

"Well, he sort of threatened Dave through Laura, I guess. He told her he'd make Dave's life miserable or something like that if she didn't stop seeing him."

He made another note, also shielded from my view. "Okay, what about Jake?" he asked. "What was his story?"

I told him everything Jake had told me, and added that Jake had neglected to mention that Dave had been found in his room. He wrote all that down, too.

"Okay. You searched the apartment," Brian said, sounding as if he were trying to control his temper. "You left the passbook and calendar there but you took the printout?"

"Right."

"Where is it now?"

"The printout?" I said. "It's at my house."

"All right. We'll pick up the calendar and the passbook from the apartment and I'll send somebody by your house to get the printout."

Darn. I'd have to hurry up and copy it before they got there.

"Anything else?" he said.

I thought for a few moments, and slowly shook my head. "Not that I can think of," I said.

Brian sighed, sat forward with his elbows on the table, and rested his chin on his hands. "What is your impression so far?" he said.

I raised my eyebrows. "You mean about who did it?"

"Yes. Who do you think did it? Who do you think couldn't have done it?"

"Well, I don't know," I said. "I don't think Jake did it, even though he looks suspicious. Jake thinks it's the guys who lent Dave money."

Brian frowned. "Is there any evidence at all that these guys even exist?"

"Well, no, I guess not," I said. "Jake's the only one who seems to know anything about that."

"So you don't have any good suspects, huh, Sherlock?"

I gave him a cross between a scowl and a sneer. "Well, from what I can see," I said, "neither do you."

"Touché," Brian replied.

"So who's this Cousins guy?" I asked.

"He's a new detective," Brian said. "This is his first case."

"Oh, great," I said. I rolled my eyes and shook my head.

Brian pursed his lips, and looked like he was counting to ten. Then he leaned forward and gave me an intense look. "Beth, I want you to listen to me," he said. "I want you to stay out of this. This is not Nancy Drew. This is real life. It's dangerous. You could get hurt. You could get killed."

I sighed. I sort of appreciated the concern, although I could've done without the Nancy Drew comment. I didn't say anything for several moments.

"I can't stay out of it," I said finally. "I promised Janice and I can't let her down. It means too much to her and she's counting on me."

Brian's face turned red and I could see him tighten his jaw. "You have no business messing around in a police investigation," he said. "You're going to louse things up. You could end up destroying evidence."

"Well, so far," I said, "it looks like I found evidence the police never even noticed."

Brian shifted his position abruptly and took a few deep breaths. If I'd touched him, he probably would've felt like a piece of granite.

"Brian," I said in a not-unfriendly voice, "I don't want you to be upset with me. I don't want to fight with you about this. But just try to understand, I'm just doing a favor for a good friend. I promise I'll be careful. As soon as I even think I know who it is, I'll call you. I won't even go near him. I won't do anything on my own. I never intended to."

His face softened some as I talked, and the red tint disappeared from his cheeks. He sighed, and gave me a caring smile. "I'm sorry," he said. "I didn't mean to get so hot. I'm just worried about you. I don't think you know what you're getting into."

I shrugged and smiled back.

He reached across the table and took my hand and held it in both of his. "I want you to promise me something," he said. "I want you to keep in touch with me every step of the way. Every time you talk to someone or think of something else I want you to call me. Will you do that?"

I hesitated. "Sure," I said, a bit reluctantly. "I promise."

Brian looked as if he were about to let go of my hand, but he suddenly raised it and pressed it against his lips. He turned a light shade of pink and let it drop.

"Sorry," he said. "I don't know why I did that."

I laughed. "It's all right," I said. "I didn't mind."

He gave me a shy smile. "Let's get out of here," he said. "I have to get back to work."

As soon as I got home, I pulled the printout from my file and started copying it.

"What are you doing?" Emily said.

"I'm copying the computer printout I found in Dave's room. I just had lunch with Brian McHenry and he says I have to give it to him."

Emily colored slightly and bent over her work. Janice gave me a quizzical look. I raised an eyebrow and shrugged.

It must have taken me a good forty minutes to copy the darn thing. I folded it up, placed it in a folder I marked "Brian McHenry", and put the copy in my file.

I didn't feel like working. I had Dave on my mind. "I'll be in the other room if you need me," I said. I picked up the file and went to the kitchen.

I looked through everything I had, and made a "to do" list:

—*call Dick Burghoff*
—*interview other tenants*
—*call Mr. VanderHayden?*

I picked up the phone and dialed Dick Burghoff's number. "Hello?" someone said.

"Could I speak to Dick Burghoff, please?" I said.

"This is Dick."

"Hi. I'm Beth Hartley," I said, and told him why I was calling.

"I'll tell you one thing," he said. "I never believed Dave killed himself. He had no reason. And he wasn't like that, anyway. Nothing bothered him. He didn't let things get to him."

"It seems like everyone who knew him feels the same way," I said. "Did he talk to you about what was going on in his life, other than wrestling?"

"Sure, some," Dick said.

"Do you know if he was in any kind of trouble?"

A slight hesitation. "Like what?" he asked.

"Anything," I said. "Did he ever say anything about owing anyone a lot of money, for instance?"

"No, he never said anything like that," Dick said. "But he did seem a little low on funds sometimes. He borrowed money from me a couple of times, but it was just a few bucks."

"Did he seem like he was worried about money?"

"Are you kidding? The guy never worried about anything. He just figured everything would work out somehow and it usually did, for him. Last time I lent him a twenty he said he was going to have a thousand of 'em in another week. He probably would have, too, if he hadn't died."

I frowned. "When did he say that?" I said. "Do you remember?"

"Yeah, it was the Friday before he died."

"Did he tell you where he was going to get all that money?"

"No, he never said. Look," Dick said, "he might not have been serious anyway. He was always talking like that. Like he thought he was going to be the next Donald Trump or somebody. He was just that kind of guy."

"Okay. Is there anything else that you can think of?" I asked. "Anything that was bothering him? Anyone angry at him for anything?"

Dick thought for a few moments. "No," he said. "I'm sorry, I really can't."

150   *Kathleen Anne Barrett*

"If you do think of something, would you give me a call?"

"Sure thing," he said, and I gave him my number.

"Oh, I almost forgot," I said. "Do you know if he used anything to get his weight down for wrestling?"

No answer.

I told him why I was asking.

"Oh, wow," Dick said under his breath. "Yeah, he used them. Everybody does. It gets your weight down real quick. 'Course, it goes right back up again but all you need it for is when you weigh in."

"Do you think anyone else knew he was taking them?"

"Heck, yeah," he said with a laugh. "Anyone on the team would've known. Heck, Coach probably even knows."

I sighed. "Okay, thanks, Dick. You've been a big help."

"No problem," he said.

I went back to the library and got to work. Mrs. Gunther poked her head in an hour later and said a policeman was at the door. Emily and Janice exchanged looks, and raised their eyebrows at me.

"He's just here to pick up the printout," I said with a laugh. I grabbed the file and went to the door, had a nice chat with the guy, turned over the evidence, and went back to work. I was still slightly peeved. That was my own personal evidence that I found with my own ingenuity and I didn't feel like giving it up. I knew I was being totally unreasonable, but that's how I felt.

Brian McHenry called me a couple of hours later.

"Hey, didn't they teach you in law school you're not supposed to doodle on the evidence?" he said.

"Oh, no!" I said, turning bright red. "I'm sorry. I wasn't thinking about it when I did that. Does it really matter?"

He laughed. "Don't worry about it," he said. "You behaving yourself?"

"Yes, I'm behaving myself," I said, making no effort to hide my irritation. "I just talked to another one of Dave's friends, though. A guy named Dick Burghoff."

"Beth . . . never mind. What'd the guy say?"

I told him.

"Spell his name for me."

I did.

"Number?"

I gave it to him and he sighed. "Were you planning to call me and tell me this or did I just luck out by calling you?"

"I was going to call you," I said. "I just hadn't gotten around to it yet."

"Okay," Brian said. "I have to go. Talk to you later. And be careful," he added quickly.

"I will," I said. "I promise."

The next day was Tuesday, January fifth. I worked hard, all day, and Emily stayed late because Phil was out of town for the next week. At six, seven Boston time, I decided to call Mr. VanderHayden. I left Emily in the library and took my "Dave" file to the kitchen.

I dialed the number, praying the Senator was home in Boston rather than off legislating in Washington, D.C. A maid answered.

"Whom shall I say is calling?" she said when I asked for the Senator.

"My name is Beth Hartley," I said. "I'm a friend of the family of Dave Grezinski, that's G-r-e-z-i-n-s-k-i, and I'd like to talk to Senator VanderHayden about his death."

It was a good five minutes before he came to the phone, something I suspected he did intentionally. Intimidation? Putting me in my place? Stalling so he could come up with a good story?

"This is Senator VanderHayden," he said. His voice was deep and resonant, like a bass singer's. Beautiful, really. A voice like that must command a lot of attention.

"Senator VanderHayden, my name is Beth Hartley," I said. "I'm a close friend of Dave Grezinski's sister and I'm helping her investigate his possible murder."

"And how does that concern me?" he said. His tone was cold and unfeeling, but I detected a hint of caution.

"I understand you didn't want Dave seeing your daughter, Laura," I said.

No response.

"Is that true?" I said.

I heard him sigh. "Frankly, my dear young woman, I fail to see how that concerns you. Nor do I see how that relates to the young man's death."

"Well . . . I'm not sure if it relates, either," I said. "But I'm looking for people who might have had a motive to kill him."

"I see," he said, after hesitating a few moments. "My dear young lady, the mere fact that I did not want my daughter dating the boy is hardly a motive for murder. I found him wholly unsuitable, but I certainly had no reason to take his life. Your suggestion is utterly absurd, and quite frankly, slanderous. I can assure you, young lady, that if you profess your views to anyone else, I will turn the matter over to my attorneys."

"I never said you did it, Mr. VanderHayden. I never even expressed the opinion that you did it, and an opinion wouldn't even be slanderous anyway. Besides that, you're a public figure so you don't have a chance. You'd be wasting your attorney's time." I knew I was being childish, but he really ticked me off.

I heard him take a deep breath and let it out. "Do not call me again," he said, and hung up.

What a jerk! This time I did call Brian right away, but he wasn't there so I left a message for him to call me.

I went back to the library, still working to control my anger.

"You want to go out for a pizza?" I said to Emily.

She raised her head, and gave me a puzzled look. "Sure," she said. "What's the matter with you?"

"Oh, nothing," I said. "I just talked to a real jerk. Senator VanderHayden from Boston, Massachusetts." I was using the same sort of voice Jake had used when he'd first told me about him and I smiled at myself when I realized it.

"You want to go to Balistreri's?" I said. "You won't have so far to go home, then. We can take both cars."

"Sure," she said, and packed up her stuff.

Balistreri's is in Wauwatosa, on Sixty-eighth and Wells. They don't take reservations, so you usually have to wait, but it's really worth it. The pizza's the best I've ever had. Really thin crust. It's just perfect. I'm never satisfied with anyone else's pizza anymore.

I followed Emily there so we arrived at the same time, but we had to park a block apart. The wait was short and we got a table in the back room near the window. We ordered a large pizza with about a hundred toppings and a pitcher of Coke.

"So, how was Brian McHenry?" she asked, without looking up. She seemed uncharacteristically absorbed in rearranging her silverware, seeing how many permutations she could come up with.

"He's fine," I said. "Really nice. It was pretty weird seeing him after all these years, though. I never would've recognized him."

She looked up then, smiling. "Yeah, I felt the same way when I saw him. He got so tall, for one thing."

I laughed. "Yeah, he said he grew six inches in one year. He turned out pretty good-looking, too."

She nodded, and gazed across the room at the other customers. "Did he say anything about me?" she asked, her eyes still roving the room.

"He asked how you were. He seemed glad that you were happily married."

Emily gave me a strange look, a mixture of annoyance and confusion.

"Well, you didn't want me to tell him you're having problems, did you?" I said.

She let out a deep sigh. "No, I guess not," she said. "I don't know."

"You're still hung up on him, aren't you?"

Emily's face got a little red and her eyes looked kind of glassy. "No . . . yes," she said. "No. No, I'm not. What's the point, anyway? It's too late now. He's all yours, if that's what you're after."

"I wasn't even thinking about that," I said. "I guess he

would be kind of nice to go out with but I wasn't thinking about it, and if it would bother you I wouldn't do it.''

She shook her head, still averting her eyes. ''It wouldn't bother me,'' she said quietly. ''Go ahead if you want to. He'd be perfect for you, actually.'' She looked at me then. ''I think he'd be just your type.''

I smiled. ''Really?'' I said. ''Why?''

She shrugged. ''He's genuine,'' she said. ''Real. Like you. And he's really nice, not just to people who are close to him but to everyone. He's just what you need. You're two of a kind, really.''

I had to fight against the lump I felt in my throat. I took a deep breath and smiled, then leaned forward.

''Well, you know something,'' I said. ''You may not realize it, but I think Phil is perfect for you. And I think you love him as much as he loves you. You just fight it, he doesn't. He doesn't have your history. You're so afraid of losing someone that you put up barriers. You create obstacles to keep the relationship from getting anywhere in the first place. You'd rather not have it at all than have it and lose it.''

Emily burst into tears. Oh, great, I did it again.

''Oh, Em, I'm sorry,'' I said. She put her hand to her head and shielded her face, hoping to keep other people from seeing her. It didn't work. At least three tables of customers were staring at us.

''I'm sorry,'' she said in a few minutes. ''I know you're right, that's all. I just wish I knew what to do about it.''

''Well, don't ask me. I have the same problem.''

She started laughing then, and *everyone* was looking at us. ''We're hopeless, you know that?'' she said.

I gave her a tell-me-about-it look. ''Let's get out of here,'' I said.

All the way home, I thought about Senator VanderHayden and the conversation I'd had with him. The guy was such a jerk, and he really made me kind of nervous. I told myself I was being silly, though. He was halfway across the country, in Boston. What could I possibly have to worry about?

Chapter Twelve

It was almost ten when I got home. The air was bitterly cold, the sky a mass of swiftly moving clouds ranging in hue from dirty gray to ugly black. Broken branches were flying about and one of my next-door neighbor's trash cans had blown over. I put the car in the garage, took a cup of tea and a book up to bed, read for about an hour, and turned off the light.

The next day was Wednesday, January sixth. It was snowing lightly when I woke up but the forecast was ten inches. I went downstairs to make breakfast and discovered I had a bit of grocery shopping to do. I'd have to do it early, too, before the snow got too deep. I scrounged around for something to eat, waited for Janice, Emily, and Mrs. Gunther to arrive, and told them I'd be back in about an hour, that I had some errands to run.

I loaded up on food, and restocked my liquor supply with some Scotch, tequila, a quart of vodka, and some Jim Beam whiskey (I don't actually drink any of that stuff but it's good to have for guests). The snow was coming down fast now, big flakes that were so close together they nearly formed a sheet. Peter was out shoveling, poor kid, barely able to keep ahead of the fall. I told him not to bother. He could come back tomorrow after it'd stopped. He flashed me a grateful grin, scooped up some snow, and made a snowball, which he playfully threatened to throw at my head.

"Never throw snowballs at the people who pay you," I said.

I hung my wet clothes in the mudroom, set the liquor on the kitchen table, and put the rest of the groceries away.

155

I was just about to go into the library when the phone rang. It was Jake.

"Some cops were here last night," he said. "They took that calendar and savings book out of Dave's desk."

"Oh, yeah," I said. "I forgot they were going to do that. I should've warned you. Sorry."

"That's okay," he said. "I sort of freaked when I opened the door, though."

I laughed. "I'll bet," I said. "So how've you been? You getting your packing done?"

"Yeah, pretty much. I'm still trying to find another place, though. I might be stuck here another month."

"Are you looking for one with a roommate?" I asked.

"Yeah," Jake said. "I really can't afford it by myself. Why? You know someone?"

"No, but if I hear of anyone I'll let you know."

"Thanks," he said. "So, how's it going with you? You getting any leads yet?"

"No, not really. I found out he was expecting to make a lot of money about the time he died, though. Did he say anything to you about that?"

"Naw," Jake said. "He didn't say anything like that."

"Okay, well, thanks, Jake. I'll talk to you soon. I'll let you know if I figure anything out."

"Okay, catch you later," he said. "Let me know if I can help."

"I will," I said with a smile. He'd warmed up a lot since I'd first met him and I was really beginning to like him.

I worked the rest of the day, sent everyone home at three because of the snow, and Tony called at five-thirty.

"Hi," he said softly, sending my heart aflutter. "You snowed in over there?"

I laughed. "I sure am," I said.

"Me, too," he said. "Luckily, most of my patients canceled so I got home before it was too late. I got stranded at the office once last year."

"Wonderful," I said.

"You doing anything Friday night?" Tony asked.

"Nope," I said. "What'd you have in mind?"

"A little dinner? Maybe Fox & Hounds if the weather's not too bad?"

"I'd love it," I said. "That's one of my favorite restaurants." Fox & Hounds is a great German restaurant in the Kettle Moraine, near Holy Hill.

"Mine, too," he said. "I'll tell you what. I'll call you early Friday, when we know what the weather's going to be like and if it's too bad for Holy Hill we'll go somewhere in town."

"Okay, great," I said. "I'll talk to you on Friday."

I made myself a cup of tea after we hung up, and sat at the kitchen table watching the snow. Its pace had picked up considerably, which excited me no end. Ever since I can remember, I've been mesmerized by big snowstorms, elated at the thought of being snowed in, all cozy and warm inside while great mounds of white stuff enveloped my house.

When I was little, my father told me stories of growing up in northern Wisconsin, where the snow was so deep it sometimes covered the windows. Once, my dad said, it was so high he was able to climb to the top of the drift and just step onto the roof. I wonder now if he was telling me the truth. He once told my brother that Fritos were made from pigskin.

I went into the library and knit for a couple of hours, made myself some dinner, and decided to finish my laundry. I went upstairs, piled at least three loads' worth into a basket, brought it down to the basement, turned on the radio, and started sorting. Ooh, Rachmaninoff's second piano concerto was on. I put the first load in, cranked up the radio, and listened to the whole thing before I went back up the stairs.

I couldn't get the basement door open.

I pushed on it with all my strength, trying several times, but it wouldn't budge. And then I saw the smoke. Little wisps at first, then great curling clouds. It was coming under my basement door and there was no way out. The windows were too small. Mere slits no grown human being could ever fit through. My house was on fire! I started to panic. I was coughing and the smoke was burning my eyes. I looked around frantically for a way out, but there was no escape.

The clothes chute! I could go through the clothes chute! I'd crawled through once as a kid. I could do it again. I pulled on the door. It wouldn't open. I yanked on it as hard as I could, but it still wouldn't move. I ran downstairs, grabbed a screwdriver, and came back up. I pried around the edges, trying to loosen it up. I put the screwdriver down, and tried again. It opened! I put my palm on the other door. It was hot. My kitchen was on fire! I'd be escaping into the fire rather than out. I panicked again. What the heck was I going to do? If I stayed down here, I'd surely die. I had no choice. I had to get out. I pushed on the second door. It was stuck too. I ran down the stairs, again, and got a hammer. I ran back up, and banged on the door as hard as I could, hitting it around the edges. It seemed like hours went by, but finally it opened, heat and smoke blasting me in the face. It was hideously hot, but the fire was still some distance away from the chute. I decided to go for it.

It wasn't until that moment that I considered the size of the opening.

The chute couldn't be more than fifteen inches wide, maybe sixteen at the most. I tried to get through, but the fit was too snug. Now what was I going to do? All I needed was a little more room, just a little. The smoke was so dense I could hardly breathe. The heat was almost unbearable. I pulled my shirt over my face, coughing and crying, my mind racing for something to do.

I had it! I took off all my clothes and tried again. It was *still* too tight—darn! I ran downstairs, grabbed a bottle of laundry detergent, and ran back up. I greased myself from neck to toes, wiped my hands on my clothes, and tried again. This time, I got my shoulders through. I was halfway there, now for the hips. I could've sworn they were the same width as my shoulders. But they wouldn't go through. I was stuck.

I felt faint and sick to my stomach. The heat and smoke were suffocating me. There wasn't any air to breathe and I was weaker by the minute. I knew I'd die if I didn't get out. I had to try one more time. I grabbed the outside door and pulled with every ounce of strength I could muster. The last thing I remember is making it through, screaming with pain, and then everything went blank.

When I came to, I was in the back of an ambulance, wrapped in blankets, with All-Purpose Cheer smeared all over my body. The fire department was there, as well as the police, and my next-door neighbor, Marie, who'd reported seeing the smoke. I was taken to the hospital, given all kinds of tests and treatments, and released at one the next day. I called Marie (to save alarming anyone who didn't already know), begged her to bring me some clothes, and went home in her car. When she pulled up in front of my house, I started to cry. I couldn't see any of the damage from the front, but the place was swarming with people, investigating who knows what and invading whatever privacy I had left. All I wanted was to be alone, in my own bed, with no one to bother me.

Brian was standing in my living room when I walked in. The look on his face was so tender I just ran into his arms and sobbed into his chest. He stroked my hair, kissed the top of my head, then walked me over to the couch and sat down beside me with his arm around my shoulders.

"How're you feeling?" he said in a gentle voice.

"Awful," I said, and started to cry again. Every inch of my body hurt. My shoulders and hips were bruised and scraped. My head felt like the housing for a kettledrum. I hadn't even seen my face and I was afraid to look.

"Emily and your secretary were here . . ."

"Oh, no!" I said. "Janice and Emily. I forgot all about them."

"It's okay," Brian said. "I told them what happened and said you'd call them when you felt up to it."

"Thanks," I said. "Janice is Dave's sister, you know."

Brian nodded. "She told me. She's blaming herself for what happened."

I looked at Brian and frowned. "What do you mean?" I said. "Why would she blame herself for this?"

Brian gave me a puzzled look. "I assumed you knew," he said. "Someone deliberately set the fire."

I closed my eyes and took a deep breath. "I guess I really did know," I said. "I just didn't want to believe it."

Brian sighed, and took my fingers in his. "I hope you're going to stop all of this now," he said. "You could've been killed last night. Whoever did this *meant* to kill you." He gave me the most pleading look and waited for my response.

I didn't know what to say. I couldn't quit. He should've known that. On the other hand, what was left for me to do?

"I don't know what else I would've done anyway," I said. "I've already talked to everyone I can think of who might know something." (Of course, if someone or something else came to mind, I'd surely pursue it. But I didn't have to tell Brian that.)

Brian let out a big sigh, and smiled. "Thank you," he said.

"Oh, I just remembered," I said. "I talked to Laura VanderHayden's father. I forgot to tell you about that." I winced. "Sorry."

Brian shook his head as if to say *Forget it.* "What did he say?"

I told Brian everything, including Mr. VanderHayden's threat to call his attorneys.

"Where's your phone?"

"In the ki . . . in the library," I said. "I'll show you."

"No," he said quickly. "Don't get up. Just tell me where it is."

He came back a few minutes later, and sat down again.

"How long have these guys been here?" I asked.

"Since early this morning. They'll be here a while yet."

"Darn," I said.

Brian put his hand on my knee. "Hold on," he said. "I'll see if I can find out how long they're going to be."

He came out less than a minute later, with another man, who was carrying four clear plastic bags tied with string.

"Ma'am," the man said. "My name is John Clancy. I'm an arson investigator." He showed me the bags, and asked if I recognized the contents.

I frowned, and nodded in confusion. "That's the liquor I bought yesterday."

"Were they empty before the fire, ma'am?"

"No," I said. "They were full. I never opened them."

He nodded, and addressed Brian. "Looks like the accelerant," he said. He looked at me again. "We detected alcohol with a chromatograph, on your kitchen table and in front of the basement door. Whoever started this fire, ma'am, used your alcohol to fuel it. That and the newspapers you had piled up in your mudroom. Do you remember where the alcohol was before the fire?"

"I left it on the kitchen table," I said, and started to cry. Brian gave the investigator a silent signal and he left us alone.

He sat me down on the couch again and put his arm around my shoulders. When I stopped crying, he asked me if I felt up to telling him what I could remember.

"Can it wait?" I said. "I already went through the whole thing for the police who came to the hospital. I don't want to have to think about it again right now."

"Sure," Brian said. "It can wait. These guys will probably be here another hour or so. I'll stay with you until they leave if you want me to."

"Thanks," I said, and rested my head against his arm.

"Hey, remember John Schroeder?" Brian said. "The one who was a new kid in fifth grade and then he left the next year? The one who was always brushing his teeth in the bathroom after lunch?"

I laughed (which hurt, by the way). "Yeah, I think so," I said. "Why?"

"He's a dentist now."

I laughed even harder then, which hurt even more. Brian went on like that, telling me anecdotes about our former classmates, none of whom I'd seen or heard of in all those years, until everyone was gone. When the last of them left, Brian stood up.

"I have to go," he said. "You ought to try to get some sleep and put it out of your mind. I'll call you tomorrow."

I got up, too, and gave him a big hug. He hugged me back and we stood there for several minutes, neither of us wanting to break away first. He finally did, gave me a kiss on the top of my head, and said good-bye.

As I walked upstairs, I heard the phone ring but I let it go. I couldn't wait to get into bed. There's nothing like being in your own bed, all snuggled under the covers, to make the goblins go away. I took a painkiller, pulled my quilt over my head, and fell fast asleep.

The smoke was blacker and thicker this time, and the flames were out of control. I was naked again and I was frantic. I crawled through the hot metal maze, searching for a way out, but every opening was a doorway of flames. Fiery tendrils reached deep into the chute, snatching and grasping, scorching my flesh. I screamed, shrinking back, and they only reached farther.

I sat upright in bed, drenched in sweat, trembling all over, and I started to cry. I stayed in that position, wide awake, for the rest of the night.

The next day I did nothing but sleep, not even bothering to eat. Janice called, said she'd warned Mrs. Gunther not to come, and asked if I needed anything. She was beside herself with guilt and I didn't have the energy to make her feel better. Emily called, then Tony, whom I'd completely forgotten about. He was shocked when I told him what had happened, offered to come over to do anything he could, but I said no. He gave me a rain check on our dinner date and asked me to call him when I felt up to it. Brian called, asked how I was doing, and promised to call again the next day.

I woke up Saturday morning, feeling like I could eat a seven-course meal. The last nourishment I'd had was on Thursday morning before I left the hospital, and *it* was awful.

I called Emily. "How would you like to meet me at Ma Fischer's?" I said. "I don't have a kitchen anymore and I'm starving to death."

"I'll be right there," she said.

I took a quick shower, wincing every time I touched myself, and looked in the mirror for the first time since I'd come home. The sides of my body were black and purple, abrasions stretching from the pelvic bone halfway down my thighs. My face was a mess, with a large violet lump on my forehead, and something that looked like a blistering sunburn across one of my cheeks. I drew in my breath, tears stinging my eyes.

I didn't have any liquid makeup to cover it because I never wear the stupid stuff. I tried powder instead but it actually looked worse. I washed it off and left it the way it was. I put on baggy sweats to minimize the friction, and went.

I got there before Emily and took a booth as far away from the door as I could get. Ma Fischer's is an old, home-style place on Farwell, just south of North Avenue, open twenty-four hours a day. We used to go there for breakfast a lot, after a night on the town. I ordered coffee, and was sipping it with my head down when Emily came in.

When I lifted my head, she gasped and actually got tears in her eyes.

She sat down and gingerly touched my arm. "Are you all right?" she said, her voice breaking.

I smiled weakly. "Yeah, I guess," I said. "It could've been a lot worse."

"I don't know how you could be so stupid," Emily said.

I closed my eyes. "Please, Emily," I said, tears welling up. "Give me a break, at least for today."

"I'm sorry," she said, and sounded like she meant it. She even looked guilty. Maybe near brushes with death would be good for her, as long as they were mine.

We had omelettes and sausage, drank over a pot of coffee between us, and even had dessert. We walked to the corner and browsed through the Oriental Drugstore for a while, and then decided to go to Emily's. We stopped on the way to drop off my car, and drove to her place in hers. I stayed the rest of the day, and night, and for the first time since it happened, I got a really good night's sleep. I remembered to call Mrs. Robinson while I was there, told her I'd been hurt, but not how badly, and we decided to postpone our visit until the next week. I reminded her, again, to keep her door closed and locked. It's a good thing I did, because she had forgotten. She had to go and shut it while we were still on the phone.

Emily brought me home early Sunday morning, and came in with me. I hadn't seen my kitchen yet and didn't want to experience it alone. We went in the front door, crossed through the living room into the dining room, and gasped, both at the same time.

The dining room was untouched, except for some water damage, but the kitchen was a total disaster. The whole room was a sooty, sodden mess. The curtains were gone, the linoleum blistered and buckled, the wallpaper blackened and seared. In the center of my kitchen table was a shiny black scar, with a succession of black marks extending from it in a pattern that looked like alligator skin.

I stepped gingerly through the room, with Emily behind me, went into the mudroom, and stared, open-mouthed, at the basement door. A large "V" was burned into its surface and the floor beneath it was black and blistered. The mudroom itself was destroyed, the wallpaper burned off, wooden coat hooks gone, the small chest, where I'd kept hats and scarves, completely ruined. The memory of the fire and the fear that went with it came back in a rush. I wondered if I'd ever have the nerve to go down those basement stairs again. I shut the door, walked out of the kitchen to the living room, and sank down on the couch.

"Good grief, what a mess," Emily said. "Did the insurance company come out yet?"

I nodded with my eyes closed.

"What's the damage estimate?"

"I don't know yet," I said. "And I don't care, as long as they pay it." I shook my head. "I'm glad my Aunt Sarah isn't here to see this."

"Yeah, I know what you mean," Emily said. "Well, look at it this way. At least you can finally get rid of that hideous wallpaper."

I opened my eyes and laughed. "Hey, you're right," I said. "You know, I actually had a nightmare about that wallpaper once? The spoons were chasing me all over the house and they had big hands and feet and really mean, ugly faces.''

"Pretty spooky," Emily said. "When was that?"

"When I was seven or eight, I think."

She laughed. "Well, now you can redecorate the whole kitchen, furniture and all, and it won't cost you a cent."

"Yeah," I said, grinning. "I can buy an Ethan Allen table and china cabinet and maybe get ceramic tile this time. I've always wanted ceramic tile."

"You'd better curb your enthusiasm a bit or they'll think you torched the place yourself."

"Yeah, right."

"Well, are you going to be okay?" Emily said.

I nodded.

"Okay, I'm going to get going but I'll call you later. Maybe we can go out to dinner somewhere."

"Great," I said. "I guess I'll be eating out for quite a while, huh?"

"Hey, live it up," Emily said. "I'll talk to you later."

I went to the library, sat at my desk, and took out my "Dave" file. I hadn't even opened it when I heard someone banging on my door.

It was Jake.

"I found something," he said breathlessly. "I found something in the apartment."

I pulled him in and closed the door.

"What the heck happened to you?" he said when he saw my face. He frowned, and wrinkled his nose. "Do you smell smoke?"

"Someone set fire to my house," I said.

Jake took a step back and whipped his head around, looking frantically about the room.

"Not now, Jake. Wednesday. That's where this came from," I said, pointing to my face.

"Oh," he said, looking relieved. "Do they know who did it?"

"No," I said, "but my guess is it's the same person who killed Dave."

"Holy cow," Jake said, his eyes bugging out. He sat down on the couch with his mouth open.

"I'd offer you something to drink," I said, "but the fire was set in my kitchen so I don't have anything."

"Oh, no problem," he said.

"So, what did you find?" I said. He'd been holding a business-sized envelope in his hands, fingering it nervously and bending it around the edges.

"This," he said, thrusting it toward me. "I found it under Dave's mattress when I took the sheets off."

I frowned. "Why'd you take the sheets off?"

"Because they were mine," he said, clearly annoyed.

I removed the letter from the envelope and unfolded it. There was only one page. No letterhead. Just plain, white, heavy bond. No date on the letter. Illegible postmark on the envelope. It was to Dave, from Laura's father. A check was enclosed, the letter said, to be cashed in exchange for Dave's agreement to stop seeing Laura. There was no reference to the amount of the check, and the check was no longer in the envelope.

"It has to be him," Jake said when I'd finished reading it. "He must've found out Dave was still seeing her and he killed him because he cashed his lousy check." Jake's jaw and both fists were clenched. "Senator Lowlife," he said.

"Jake," I said. "Do you know Dave cashed the check?"

He gave me a look like my head was ten feet thick. "Of course he cashed it," he said. "It's not in the envelope."

"He could've sent it back," I said. "He could've torn it up. Maybe he put it somewhere else."

"Oh," Jake said, looking dejected.

"This is still a very important piece of evidence no matter what he did with the check," I said.

Jake's face brightened up and he gave me a wistful smile.

"I think you should take this to the police," I said. "I'll go with you if you want."

He nodded, grinning. "Cool," he said. "Let's do it."

I called Brian at home. "Jake Grossman found something in the apartment I think you'll be interested in," I told him, winking at Jake. Jake grinned like a little kid.

"I'll be right over," Brian said.

A half-hour later, Brian was in my living room, removing the letter from its envelope, holding it at the very tip of one corner. Jake and I exchanged a look.

"How'd you happen to find this?" Brian asked Jake when he'd returned the letter to the envelope.

Jake explained, got thoroughly interrogated, and explained some more. I was getting really ticked off at Brian for giving him such a hard time. The poor kid was just trying to help.

Emily called later that evening and we went out to dinner, this time to T. G. I. Friday's. The bump on my head had gone down a lot and I'd bought some liquid makeup to cover the scrapes and bruises. If the lighting was right, I looked almost human.

"Jake Grossman came over today," I told her. "He found a letter to Dave from Laura's dad. The guy actually bribed him to stay away from his daughter, can you believe that?"

"You're kidding!" Emily said. "How much?"

"I don't know," I said. "The check was gone and it didn't say how much in the letter."

"You mean the little creep cashed it?"

"Who knows?" I said. "He could've sent it back, for all I know."

"Yeah, that's true," Emily said. "What about this Jake guy, though? Don't you ever wonder about him? I mean, he finds the body, right? He doesn't tell the cops, he takes off for days, doesn't even show up for the funeral, and the body's found in his room with a note on his typewriter."

I sighed. "Yeah, I know what it looks like," I said, "but I still don't think he did it."

"Why not?" Emily said.

"I don't know. Just a gut feeling, I guess. I really like him. He's so funny, he gets all these really crazy ideas about who did it, and he was so excited about finding that letter, like he thought he was going to solve the case and become famous or something.''

Emily gave me a skeptical look. ''How do you know it's not just an act?'' she said.

''Well, I don't know for sure,'' I said. ''I just don't think he did it, that's all.''

''Okay, okay,'' Emily said. ''I'm just trying to help. But don't you think it . . .''

I shot her a warning look.

''Just one more thing and then I'll shut up,'' she said.

I waited.

''Don't you think it's strange that the note was typed on a typewriter instead of a computer? Dave's supposed to be this computer wizard, right? And the note's supposed to be written by him, so why's it written on a typewriter?'' She sat back with a smug look on her face.

I frowned. ''I just figured the killer was in a hurry and a typewriter was faster. He wouldn't have to print it out, for instance.''

''Yeah . . . or maybe the killer doesn't know how to use a computer.''

My eyebrows shot up.

''Does Jake know how to use one?'' Emily said.

I groaned. ''No, but neither do I. Neither do you. Where does that get us?''

''It's better than nothing,'' she said. ''Of all the people you talked to, which ones do you know of who don't know how to use a computer?''

I thought for a moment. ''I don't know,'' I said. ''I didn't ask anyone that. I know Jake and Tony don't but I didn't ask Laura, or Laura's father, or Dr. King, or Dave's friends, or . . .''

''Okay, you made your point.''

''Brian thinks the guy could've been after something I have in the house, or something he thinks I have.''

''Why does he think that?'' Emily said.

''Because of the fire, I guess. Maybe he thought the fire would destroy whatever it was.''

Emily shrugged.

"The thing is, he used the liquor I left on the kitchen table to start the fire, which makes it look like he might not have intended to set a fire and maybe just got the idea on the spur of the moment."

"Hmm, good point," Emily said. "What were you doing in the basement?"

"Laundry. I was only down there about fifteen or twenty minutes but I had the radio on so I didn't hear anyone come in."

"So there's no way this person could've known you'd be down there when he decided to come over, right?"

"Right," I said. "Yeah, so he decides to come over planning to do who knows what and hears me in the basement and gets the idea to set the fire and lock me in."

Emily shuddered. "How did he get in to begin with?" she said.

"I don't know. It had to be through the back door. The front was deadbolted. There wasn't any damage to the back door, though, but he could've picked the lock, I guess. Or maybe I just forgot to lock it. I do that sometimes."

"Why don't you get a deadbolt for the back door?" Emily said.

"I never thought I needed it. The lock worked fine. Besides, I hate having to use a key to unlock it from the inside. They always put that kind in when there's a window in the door and I don't think it's safe. What if there's a fire or something and you can't get out because you don't have the key?"

Emily gave me an exasperated look. "Do you really feel safe with it the way it is?" she said.

"No," I said with a sigh. "I guess you're right. I'd better get one."

Boy, was that a mistake.

Chapter Thirteen

The next day was Monday, January eleventh. Janice, Emily, and Mrs. Gunther showed up, and we all worked a regular day, except we had to go out to lunch and Mrs. Gunther didn't have to clean the kitchen.

I had a locksmith come over and install a deadbolt in the back door, the kind that requires a key to get out—the kind I don't like—but I did feel a lot better when he was through. He convinced me a bolt that didn't need a key would be a waste of time because an intruder could just break the glass, reach in, and undo it. I guess they know what they're doing. I had him put a new one on the front door, too.

"If you don't mind my saying so, ma'am, you ought to get a security system installed. They're priced reasonable nowadays and they're well worth the trouble," he said.

I gave the man a weak smile. "You're probably right," I said. "Maybe I need one of those, too."

As soon as he left, I made some calls, priced a few systems, and arranged to have someone come out the following week. I'd turn the place into a fortress before I was through.

Emily went back out again, right after lunch, and returned almost two hours later with a cooler, a small automatic coffeemaker, coffee, filters, non-dairy creamer, disposable plates, cups, and utensils, napkins, trash bags, cereal, tea bags, instant soup, crackers, Jiffy Pop popcorn, and a hotplate! The cooler was full of ice, soda, fruit, and cheese.

My lip trembled and tears filled my eyes. "Thank you," I said, and hugged her until she pushed me away.

170

"Cut it out. You're getting me all wet," she said with a laugh.

Later, after everyone went home, I called Jake. "You want to help me investigate?" I said.

"Sure," he said with undisguised excitement. "What do you want me to do?"

I told him about the tenants I still wanted to question. "I'd do it myself," I said, "but I don't want to run into Mrs. Robinson. I don't want her to see me until my face looks a little better, you know what I mean?"

"Yeah, you do look pretty gruesome," Jake said. "What do you want me to ask them?"

I gave him a list of questions. "Let me know what they say, okay?"

I hung up, had myself a picnic supper of cheese and crackers, fruit and tea, and ate in the dining room with my back to the kitchen. Twenty minutes later, Jake called me back.

"Okay," he said. "The only one who was home was Mrs. Seinfeld, but she says she didn't hear anything. She was home all night but she had her TV on real loud 'cause she's hard of hearing. She also told me Mrs. Duncan's in Florida and she left before it happened, so she wouldn't know anything anyway. I don't know about the others."

"Okay," I said. "Thanks, Jake."

"What do you want me to do next?" he said.

I laughed. "That's it for now, unless one of the other ones comes home. But I'll let you know if I think of anything else."

"Okay," he said. "I'll keep on it."

I called Laura next. I wanted to find out if she knew about her father's offer to Dave. I found her at home but she was on her way out.

"I have something I really need to talk to you about," I said. "Are you free at all tonight?"

"No, I'm not," she said. "I have to work. That's where I'm going now. How about tomorrow?"

"Okay. What—"

"Wait, I have an idea," she said. "You could come see me

at the mall and talk to me during my break. I could meet you at the food court.''

''Great,'' I said. ''Which mall?''

''Grand Avenue. My break's at seven-thirty. I could meet you, like in front of Chick-Fil-A? I only get a half-hour so I'll have to eat while we talk if that's okay.''

''Sure,'' I said. ''I'll see you then.''

I retouched my makeup and winced at the sight of myself, wishing I'd thought to warn Laura about my appearance. I was still wearing sweats, since nothing else was comfortable. In short, I looked horrible.

I left at seven, parked in the mall lot, and went in at the second level as I usually do. I was a few minutes early so I bought a cup of tea and sat at a table in our agreed location.

''Oh, Beth, what happened? Were you in an accident?'' Laura said when she saw me. She looked genuinely shocked, and frightened.

''Someone locked me in my basement and set fire to my house,'' I said. ''I got hurt trying to escape.''

''Oh, no,'' Laura said. She put both hands over her mouth. ''Oh, no,'' she said again.

''It's not as bad as it looks,'' I said. ''I'm all right.''

''But you could've been killed,'' she said.

I raised my eyebrows. ''I think that was the idea.''

She flinched.

''Why don't you get something to eat?'' I said with a smile.

''Okay,'' she said with uncertainty. ''Do you want anything?''

''No, thanks,'' I said.

Laura returned a few minutes later with some breaded chicken, french fries shaped like little waffles, and a lemonade.

''So what's up?'' she said after she'd taken a few bites.

I took a deep breath. ''Jake Grossman found a letter to Dave from your dad,'' I said.

She stopped chewing for a moment and stared at me. ''What kind of letter?'' she said as she resumed eating.

I hesitated, not knowing how she'd take it. ''He asked Dave to stop seeing you and he offered him money to do it.''

The look on her face was a mixture of pain, and maybe confusion, and I don't know what.

"I'm sorry," I said. "I wasn't sure if you knew."

She didn't respond, just lowered her eyes and shredded a napkin.

"Dave never mentioned it to you?"

Laura slowly shook her head.

"I called your dad the other day," I said.

She looked up, and waited for me to continue.

"I don't think he liked me."

Laura burst out laughing. "I'm sorry," she said. "I didn't mean to laugh but it sounded so funny."

I smiled. "When did your father first tell you to stop seeing Dave?" I said.

"Thanksgiving," she said. "Right after he met him."

"There was supposed to be a check with the letter but it wasn't there when Jake found it."

Laura frowned. "You mean you think he cashed it?" she said.

"I doubt it," I said, not really believing what I was saying. "He probably just tore it up or sent it back."

Laura looked grateful and relieved. She glanced at her watch then. "Uh-oh," she said. "I have to go. I'm sorry. Was that all you wanted to tell me?"

I nodded. "Yeah, that was it," I said. "I hope I didn't upset you too much."

She shook her head. "It's not your fault," she said, and walked away.

I went home, made some notes about our conversation, and looked through my file. When I came to the bankbook notations I suddenly remembered something. I called Jake.

"Jake, I do have something else for you to do," I said.

"Sure. What?"

"There's a letter from Laura to Dave in the false bottom of that center drawer. The police didn't take it, did they?"

"I don't think so," Jake said. "Hold on, I'll check.

"Got it," he said a few minutes later. "What do you want me to do with it?"

"I hate to ask," I said, "but could you bring it over here?"

"Sure, no problem. I'll be right there."

"Did you read it?" I asked when he handed me the letter.

Jake looked a little embarrassed. "Yeah, I read it," he said. "Pretty heavy stuff."

I raised my eyebrows and removed the letter from the envelope. This one was five pages long, handwritten on both sides. There was no date on the letter but the postmark was December fifth. It had been mailed from Milwaukee.

The "heavy stuff" to which Jake referred were Laura's repeated declarations of love for Dave ("I love you more than anything in the world," "I just know we're destined to be together," and "I don't know what I'd ever do without you," to quote a few), some surprisingly detailed references to their love life (you don't really want to hear those, do you?), and complaints about Dave's refusal to verbalize his feelings. Apparently Dave was one of those wonderfully circumspect guys who says "I love you" once and then expects you to feel you don't need to hear it again. I hate that. I'd love to see how men would react if we gave them what *they* wanted only once.

The portion of the letter that interested me the most was at the top of the last page:

I told my dad there was no way I was ever going to stop seeing you. He knows I know about the check, too. You should have seen his face when I told him what you said. He is such a complete jerk. I told him if he ever tried anything like that again he'd *be the one I'd never see again.*

"Why would she lie to me?" I said, thinking out loud.

"Who?" Jake said.

"Laura. When I told her about the letter from her dad she acted like she didn't know anything about it."

Jake shrugged. "Maybe she forgot."

Yeah, or maybe she was protecting her father. But why? Talk about misplaced loyalty.

I sighed. "Well, it looks like we have another letter to show Brian McHenry," I said. "But it'll have to wait until tomorrow."

Tuesday, January twelfth. I called Brian, first thing, but he wasn't there so I left a message asking that he return my call. We worked all day, Em and Janice went home at five, and the phone rang at six o'clock.

"Sorry I didn't get back to you sooner," Brian said. "How are you feeling?"

"A lot better," I said. "My bruises keep changing color, though. It's pretty weird."

He laughed. "I'll bet," he said. "You're staying out of trouble, I hope."

"Yes, I am," I said in a mock-obedient voice. "But I do have another piece of information for you." I told him about Laura's letter.

"Okay," he said. "I was just about to leave here. Why don't I stop by and pick it up on my way home?"

"Okay. I'll see you in a little while," I said.

Brian was here in twenty minutes. He didn't say much, just asked for the letter and left. I had the feeling he was angry with me, but I couldn't be sure. I felt kind of hurt, though, and that sort of annoyed me.

I had another cheese, crackers, and fruit dinner, and sat at the dining room table paging through my file.

What if Brian was right? What if I did have something the killer wanted? Or maybe he just thought I had it. In any case, whatever it was he wanted, it probably contained the answer, or a really strong clue to the answer. Otherwise, why would he want it? Now how's that for brilliant deductive reasoning?

So, what did I have?

My own notes. That couldn't be it. Dave's monthly expenses. I read through them twice, then a third time. There was nothing the least bit unusual about them. His medical expenses? Cardiologist, dermatologist, podiatrist, dentist. Sickly kid, but big deal.

The information I'd copied from the bankbook. Now there was a possibility. Maybe the killer had given Dave money, and didn't want any evidence of the deposit lying around. I don't know; that didn't sound too plausible. Maybe Dave and the killer had some sort of illegal business going together and the killer thought the bankbook would give that away. No, stupid idea. I put the bankbook aside.

I picked up my list of the calendar entries. He did have a notation about something happening at nine o'clock on the day he was murdered, and we knew he was killed around that time. But why would the killer want the calendar? Because it was evidence of an arranged meeting? Possibly. That would show Dave knew the killer. The notation was only for the time, without any mention of a name, though. But I suppose the killer wouldn't necessarily know that. I put the calendar aside, too.

What about the letters to Dave, from Laura and her dad? What if it were Laura's dad, and he suspected I had his letter? Laura knew about it and she was protecting him. *She* must think he did it.

I dialed her number.

"Laura? This is Beth Hartley," I said when she answered the phone.

"Hi," she said. "What's up?" She sounded wary to me, but I could've been imagining it.

"I found a letter from you to Dave, in his apartment," I said. "In it, you make reference to the money your dad offered to pay Dave to stop seeing you."

Silence.

"Laura?" I said.

"Yeah?"

"Well, why didn't you tell me you knew about it?"

"I don't know," she said. "What's the difference?"

"Do you suspect your dad did it?" I said.

"Did what?" Laura said.

"Killed Dave," I said. "Do you think your dad killed Dave? Is that why you didn't tell me?"

Silence again.

"Laura, if you do," I said, "I think you're making a big mistake protecting him. Dave was someone you really loved, and your father knew that."

She started to cry then. "I have to go," she said, and hung up.

Darn. I went back to my file.

The only thing I had left to consider was the copy of the computer printout I'd found in Dave's desk. I'd never actually read through the whole thing—I hadn't seen any point and it was too long. I started to page through it then, reading every name, date, and number, hoping to trigger something. I must have gone through ten pages before I saw it.

Erma Shemanski. Mrs. Gunther's sister.

What the heck was Erma Shemanski's name doing in the computer printout?

I kept going. Eight pages later, I found it again. By the time I'd gone through the entire document, I'd picked up eleven Erma Shemanskis (twenty-two if you count the fact that every entry was printed twice). Each one was the same, except for the date. There was one duplicate entry for every month from January through November.

I sat there for a long time just thinking. Then I picked up the phone and called Mrs. Gunther. The question I asked her was whether the particular dates and numbers had any significance for her. The answer I got sent a chill through my body that caused my teeth to chatter.

I called Jake next.

"Jake, it's Beth. Do me a favor," I said. My voice was shaking so badly I could hardly talk.

"What's the matter? Are you all right?" he said.

"Look on Dave's bulletin board," I said. "I think there's an article on there about Medicaid fraud."

"Okay, hold on."

"Got it," he said.

"Read it to me."

"That's enough," I said, my voice breaking. "Hang on to that. Please, don't lose it."

"But what's . . ."

"I'll talk to you later," I said.

I started to cry, then hyperventilate. It couldn't be true. It just couldn't be him. I decided to call him.

"Well, hi, how are you?" he said in that sweet, soft voice. My heart was pounding so hard I was afraid he'd hear it over the phone.

"Oh, fine," I said. "I just felt like talking to you."

"I always feel like talking to you," he said. "Are you feeling better?"

"Yes, I am."

"Good. What are you doing?"

"Oh, nothing really," I said. "I understand you know a friend of mine. Erma Shemanski."

"Who?"

"She's one of your patients," I said. "You see her once a month."

"Is that right? I have a lot of patients. I really can't keep them all straight."

"I suppose not," I said. "That's why you hired Dave, wasn't it?"

A short hesitation. "That's right," he said. "It is. Well, what are you doing tonight?"

"Working," I said quickly. "I have a brief to write."

"How about tomorrow night? Would you like to have dinner?"

"Can I let you know tomorrow?" I said. "I might be up all night."

"Sure," he said. "Well, I won't keep you then. I'll talk to you tomorrow."

As soon as I hung up, I called Brian.

"Brian, it's Beth. I think I know who did it." I was crying and I had to stop talking to calm down.

"Take it easy," Brian said. "I'll be right over."

"Wait . . ."

"Just hang on till I get there," he said.

I hung up the phone, went into the living room, and started pacing. I was shaking so badly my muscles hurt. I had to calm down before I drove myself crazy.

I put on Bach's first piano concerto and my headphones, wrapped myself in a blanket, and lay down on the couch. Music like that can cure almost anything, even a broken heart. At the end of the first movement, I sat up, took off the headphones, and almost jumped a foot.

Tony was standing in my living room, no more than ten feet away.

"Tony!" I said. "How'd you get in here?"

He gave me a slow, smug smile and just stared for a few moments. "Same window I came through last time," he said.

"Window?" I said.

"I unlocked it when you gave me a tour of your lovely home. It's come in pretty handy."

Tears welled up and spilled from my eyes. "You set fire to my house?"

Tony shrugged. "It seemed like a good idea at the time."

I started to tremble, and pulled the blanket around my shoulders.

"Cold?" Tony said.

I nodded, sniffling.

He sat in a chair on the other side of the room, his face almost hidden by the shadows.

"You killed Dave, didn't you?" I said.

No answer.

"And you tried to kill me, too."

Still no answer.

"You left that message for me, didn't you? Why, Tony?" I said as I started to sob. "You're a doctor, you're supposed to save lives. I thought you cared about people. How could you do something like that?"

He just sat there, perfectly still, and watched me cry.

"And you've been cheating your patients," I said. "I thought they meant so much to you. You seemed so dedicated, so . . ."

"You stupid little fool," he said. "You just don't get it, do you? Can't you see I'm doing this for my patients?"

"First you overcharge them and then you kill someone? You call that helping your patients?" I said.

"My patients don't pay a cent for my services. You ought to know that. The government pays for everything. They're the ones I'm double-billing, not my patients. It's their own blasted fault for undercompensating to begin with. I only get what's rightfully mine. Without overbilling, I wouldn't be able to treat these people at all. They're indigent. Helpless. It's impossible to treat them for what Medicaid pays. Someone has to take care of them. I can't allow some—" He broke off, and sat forward in the chair, clutching the arms with both hands.

"What about your partner, Tony? Did he find out, too? Did you kill him, too?"

Tony didn't answer at first, just took a few deep breaths. "That one was regrettable," he finally said. "He, of all people, should have understood."

"Oh, Tony," I said, sobbing. "How could you?"

His face was no longer hidden in the shadows, and I could see him glaring at me, seething with loathing and anger. I probably should have kept my mouth shut, but I felt like I had nothing to lose at that point.

"You met Dave at his apartment at nine o'clock the night you killed him, didn't you?" I said.

No response.

"Was he blackmailing you? Is that why you killed him?"

Still no response.

"You paid him ten thousand dollars, didn't you?"

Tony grabbed the chair arms and yanked on them as if he were trying to pull them off.

"Shut up, you little idiot," he said. "Yes, I paid him ten thousand dollars, but he wasn't satisfied with that. He wanted more, and more. That greedy kid would've milked me for the rest of my life."

"And all this was so you could double-bill your patients?" I said. "Talk about *greed*. You're the greedy one!" I was screaming at him now, my fear overcome by my anger.

"What do you expect me to do, work for nothing?" he said. "Is that what you expect?" Now *he* was screaming, his voice growing louder with every word. "You self-righteous little . . ." He stood up and started moving toward me.

I shook my head and tried to say "No," but it wouldn't come out.

He was coming for me, but he was taking his time about it, so certain he was that I'd never get away. "You do realize, don't you," he said in the calm, soft voice I'd found so seductive only hours before, "that your own life is worth far less than the lives of all those others? It's their lives I'll be saving by taking yours."

He continued moving slowly in my direction and withdrew a syringe from his pocket. My heart leaped into my throat and I shrank back against the couch, almost paralyzed by fear. As I moved, my hand touched the headphones. I held on, having no other weapon, and waited until he was about two feet away. I flung the headphones at his face—and missed—but he ducked to avoid them, which gave me just enough time to dive over the side of the couch. I ran through the dining room and the kitchen, and then I remembered.

I didn't have the back door key!

I ran into the mudroom, down into the basement, through the first room, and into the second. Then I shut off the power.

I heard him coming down the steps. I had to find someplace to hide, but there was nothing there. A few little corners he'd have to peek around, but they'd never do for more than a few minutes. There were no windows and no furniture, just the furnace, a sink, and the washer and dryer. I lifted myself up, climbed into the dryer, and silently shut the door.

Moments later, Tony was in the room with me.

He was talking, softly calling my name, getting closer and closer all the time. Then he ran right into the dryer and banged on it with his fists.

"Come out, Beth!" he screamed. "Let's get this over with."

He was rushing around now, bumping into things, and cursing in a venomous voice.

And then I heard something else.

"Freeze!" Brian yelled.

I heard scuffling, and then a little while later, silence. I didn't move, for many minutes, until I heard Brian calling my name. I pushed open the door, and shielded my eyes from the beam of his flashlight. He lifted me out, not saying a word, and carried me upstairs.

"It's all over now; you're safe," he whispered. "It's all over."

He held me for a long time. I could feel his warm breath on my neck and his lips on my hair.

"Where's Tony?" I said a bit later.

"Outside, in a patrol car," Brian said. "I called for backup when I went for the flashlight. What happened to your power?"

"I turned it off," I said.

"You're going to need a new back door, by the way. I had to shoot the lock to get in."

I opened my mouth to say something, and shut it again.

He held me closer. "You did a darn good job, sweetheart. You ought to win a medal for this."

I laughed, and then started to cry.

"What's wrong?" he said gently.

"I don't know," I said through my tears. "I'm just relieved, I guess."

Epilogue

Three weeks later, my injuries had almost disappeared. My kitchen was looking a lot better, too. All the rubble had been cleared away, and the linoleum and old wallpaper were removed. And they'd started laying the ceramic tile. It's so cool. A really pretty terra-cotta color that blends perfectly with the wallpaper I picked out. (It's a cream background with a tiny flower print—no big spoons, nothing scary.) I ordered an eight-foot farmhouse pine table and chairs from Ethan Allen, a china cabinet with a hutch top to match, and a jelly cupboard. I can't wait till it gets here, it's so gorgeous. They're making the curtains, too—a really cute café style. The fabric's just like the wallpaper only the colors are the opposite—the background's in terra-cotta and the flowers are in cream.

I'm still upset about Tony. I feel like there's something wrong with me, that I could've been so attracted to someone like that. I've always felt I made poor choices when it came to men, but this is entering a whole new arena. The worst part is that I actually catch myself missing him—not the guy I know he is, of course, but the one I thought he was. It's almost like the Tony I liked, died.

Janice hasn't gotten over it, of course, but she's starting to feel it less, and that makes her feel guilty. I know just what she means—you do feel guilty when that happens. But I honestly think that's a built-in survival mechanism. You can't tolerate feeling that much pain, so you protect yourself emotionally, and you do it without thinking. I told her (and I really believe this) that it's the fact that she cares so *much* that makes

183

her withdraw from it. If it didn't mean so much to her she wouldn't need to do that.

Emily and Phil aren't getting along any better than they ever have. I don't know what to say about that. I saw Brian a few times. He came over to see how I was doing, and he took me to lunch, and dinner, once. I feel like I really like him, but I'm fighting it. I don't know why I can't learn to take my own advice.

I see Mrs. Robinson every Sunday and it's become my favorite part of the week. For now, I cook our suppers in her kitchen, which works out just fine. She's keeping her door open again, which really seems to make her happy—although she says she's a lot less lonely than she used to be.

Jake already moved out. He found a place, with a roommate, and grabbed it for fear of not finding another one. I really miss that kid. He gave me his new number, though, so I think I'll call him sometime and maybe take him to lunch.

Laura is doing okay. She's having a hard time being at Marquette without Dave, but she only has one semester left and she's gone. She *did* suspect her dad, she told me, and she was trying to protect him, although she doesn't know why. She says she really hated him, but he was still her dad. She feels so guilty now for having suspected him that she calls him all the time, just to talk. Funny, huh? I still think he's a jerk.

Both Emily and Brian said they hoped I learned my lesson, and won't even *think* of investigating a murder again. I don't know. Horrible as it was, I don't think I've ever felt so exhilarated, you know? I'm the one who solved it. Not the police, *me*. I don't think I could hold myself back if another one came my way. Besides, Brian said I did a darn good job of it. I take that as encouragement. Wouldn't you?